ATTACK OF THE BLACK SCORPIONS™

Don't miss our
FREE **"TEASER COMIC-BOOK" OFFER**
on page 179 !

ATTACK OF THE *BLACK* *SCORPIONS*™

A Horror-Creature Thriller

DAVID V. GREGORY

SUGGESTED FOR MATURE READERS

for INTENSE MONSTER VIOLENCE, COARSE LANGUAGE,
and ONE DETAILED LOVE SCENE

Los Angeles, California, USA

ISBN Number 979-8-9862561-1-5 (Global English Paperback Edition)

Covers designed by the author

Published by Galaxie Entertainment Company,
Los Angeles, California, USA.

This copy sold, printed, and distributed through Amazon KDP.

Dedicated to the memories of

DON CHAFFEY (1917–1990)
motion-picture director, mentor, good friend

and

PETE PETERSON (1903–1962)
superbly skilled stop-motion animator who worked
visual miracles despite an overwhelmingly painful disability.

"What we need is a story that starts out with an earthquake
and then works its way up to a climax!"

Samuel Goldwyn

THE CAST

Over three fateful nights in Southern California, many people were unwittingly caught up in the horrifying events that unfolded at and around Desert Rocks State Park. However, before we begin to recount their stories, you first need to meet them. And please be sure to enjoy their Full-Length Portraits in the Appendix.

The Principal Characters

Dan Montgomery – age 42

Dan is employed as a lineman with St. Louis Power. He's a hard worker and, with his wife Linda, scrambles against today's economy to keep his family afloat. Both a leader and team player, Dan can keep his fear in check to move forward decisively and protect everyone. Dan is husband to Linda and father to Patrick and Jennie.

Linda Montgomery – 37

A professional veterinarian, Linda works full time at the St. Louis Zoo. She pays attention to detail and loves her job – but, above all, she cares for her family. Linda totally understands and supports Dan. However, with both of them working long hours, she wishes they had more time for each other and for their son and daughter.

Patrick Montgomery – 13

Patrick may be physically challenged but he is extremely smart and amiable. As an infant, Patrick contracted an extremely rare illness. He recovered well but ended up with impaired use of his legs. Moving about on crutches or with his wheelchair and accessing the world's knowledge through his laptop computer, he manages just fine.

Jennie Montgomery – 16

Jealous of the extra attention her parents have had to give Patrick, Jennie can be short-tempered and volatile. With Dan and Linda constantly having to work, Jennie has not always had a stable role model around her. Now feeling that she is old enough to make her own decisions in life, Jennie longs for more adventures with her peers.

Tom Hernandez – 37

Tom and Yoli Hernandez are a 3rd-generation Tex-Mex couple – almost hippiesque in style and totally into crystals. A jovial family man who is always ready to welcome anyone he meets, Tom appreciates his friendships and seeks to make them stronger. Being a construction worker, Tom relates to Dan fairly well.

Yoli Hernandez – 34

Yoli complements her husband, Tom, perfectly. Sporting a blend of Southern and Tex-Mex accents, Yoli is a welcoming person – ready to make friends with anyone she encounters. She's a socializer and an organizer. Everyone is going to have a good time – whether they want to or not – and Yoli is going to see to it!

Billy Hernandez – 11

Tom and Yoli's good natures have clearly rubbed-off on their son, Billy. He's a cheerful boy who makes friends quickly. Billy is also an obedient son who doesn't mind doing chores for his parents. But when danger threatens, he can stand-up to the tasks before him – sometimes even feeling a tinge of excitement. A good friend to have.

Al Nishida – late 80's

Semi-Retired Park Ranger, Al – a 2nd-generation Japanese-American widower – is an affable fellow with a big heart who cares for all of his guests. He's as agile as a 30-year-old and doesn't let his years keep him from being active. Al adores his son's fiancée, Lauri, and looks forward to the couple blessing him with grandchildren.

Robert Nishida – 35

The park's Co-Ranger, Robert, is Al's only child. Loving nature and photography, he naturally conducts the hikes through Desert Rocks' more exotic and remote areas. Living with his father in a decaying bungalow at the park's boundary, Robert also sells nature articles and photos for extra income. Being 3rd-generation, he's pure American.

Lauri Young – 23

Robert's fiancée, Lauri is the sweet "pretty blue-eyed-blonde girl next door" who has just returned from college with a degree in conservation. Even though she always hopes for the best, Lauri easily worries over things that can affect something or someone she cares about. And she will fiercely protect what she loves.

Ken Young – 46

Lauri's parents, Ken and Joyce Young, operate a modest cattle ranch just south of the small town of Highridge and several miles north of Desert Rocks State Park. Ken is a gruff but friendly man with a strong build. He's a practical type but sometimes maybe a little too practical to see the reality of a situation until it's right on top of him.

Joyce Young – 44

Joyce is a friendly, outgoing canyon country mamma – the ideal companion for Ken. At a party in low light, you could easily mistake her for her daughter, Lauri. While she loves a good time, she's no slacker. Joyce can quickly get a handle on things when she has to.

Michael Reyes – mid-20's

Fun to be around, Michael and Elaine Reyes are on a budget honeymoon and are ready to partake in whatever Desert Rocks has to offer. They don't care where they are as long as they're together. In fact, Michael – a 2nd-generation Filipino-American – has done all the cooking on this trip so that Elaine can relax before she begins life as a homemaker.

Elaine Reyes – 19

Like all of the girls from her village, Elaine is drop-dead gorgeous and utterly unaware of it. Having migrated with her parents from an island in the central Philippines, Elaine has only been in the USA for two years. Though she'll attain citizenship through her marriage, she and Michael are madly in love and totally complete each other.

Frank Stewart – 53

Principal attorney of Richmark Oil's New York legal department and one who clearly "fell upwards" at the expense of the co-workers he stabbed in the back. Frank is a self-centered bigot who's reluctant to cooperate with anyone when he's not in control. Though he often exercises bad judgment, he <u>can</u> be resourceful if he chooses. Just give him an incentive that will be worth his time.

Margaret Stewart – 42

A former model, Margaret looks stunning for her age – but, beyond that, she's hardly ever worked a day in her life. Margaret takes care of number one and also cares greatly for her 4-year-old daughter. However, she'd sacrifice anyone to, say, drain a river so she could get across, instead of working with others to build a bridge to benefit all.

Tiffani Stewart – 4

Frank and Margaret's daughter is capable of causing trouble for anyone. Like her parents, Tiffani's learned to mostly only worry about herself. And, stirring the pot further, Frank – the dummy – doesn't know that Tiffani is not his biological child. Five years ago, Margaret successfully hid an affair from Frank, and Tiffani was the result.

Jim Johnson – mid-80's

Jim and Anne Johnson are a retired African American couple. While Indiana is home, they frequently vacation around the country in their Silverstream trailer. Jim is a good-natured and outspoken fellow who enjoys taking photos with his vintage camera. When forced into the fray, though, he will surprise you.

Anne Johnson – mid-80's

Anne is a warm relator. But she's also a thinker and, compared to Jim, a bit more reserved. Anne isn't going to go too far out of her way to offer help at first – though when asked, she will enthusiastically deliver. Anne chides Jim for being too outgoing, but she also loves him for it.

Steve Lacy – 19

Sporting leather attire and riding a classic Harley, Steve comes off as the independent bohemian type. He is intelligent, smokes dope, and is soft-spoken – though he'll put on the "tough guy" act when he deems it necessary.

Mitch Davis – 18

Mitch is liked by everyone because he's a tall, handsome, well-built African American high-school running back. Because of that, he's used to getting what he wants. It doesn't hurt that his family is well off financially, either – owning a high-end home in Baldwin Hills. His red Mustang convertible was a graduation gift from his father.

Kathy Smith – 18

Mitch's girlfriend, Kathy, is pure sweetness – never having held a malicious thought against anyone in her life. And here they are at Desert Rocks, grabbing a short vacation before starting college together in the fall. Kathy's latched on to Mitch because she thinks he's a winner. And, seeing the dollar signs, Kathy's dad thinks so too.

David Grogan – 21

David Grogan is a good-natured and friendly relator. He is at Desert Rocks for a weekend camping getaway with his college buddy, Gary Archer. Having both recently turned 21, they have strategically placed a small cooler stuffed with beer between their two pup tents.

Gary Archer – 21

Gary Archer is a friendly and outgoing socializer. He is at Desert Rocks for a weekend camping getaway with his college buddy, David Grogan. Gary has three more cases of beer stowed away in his beat-up cargo van, ready to refill their cooler at a moment's notice

Supporting Characters

Fracking Foreman – 53

Richmark Oil has hired Blackbrighton Industries to handle their fracking waste water disposal operation, and this man is the Blackbrighton junior in charge. A typical axe-man for industrial bullies, he delights in working his employees overtime and in comfortably underpaying them.

Manny – 35

Manny is the Fracking Foreman's first assistant and the wellhead operator. While he shows more common sense and humanity than his boss, Manny is intimidated by the foreman's authority and does whatever he is told.

Dr. Harold Medford II – late 80's

A truly ancient college professor, Dr. Medford is a relentless academic who has sworn to never retire. And that's fine, because he possesses an excellent mind and the laudable ability to communicate clearly. Heading the zoology and paleontology departments at UC-Riverside, he is beloved by students and faculty alike.

Additional *Incidental Characters* include **HOWARD EVANS** (Dan's Supervisor), **KEVIN** (Linda's Assistant at the Zoo), **FOUR HISPANIC OIL WORKERS**, Radio Newscaster **BUDDY MAXWELL, TWO CALIFORNIA STATE TROOPERS, THE RIVERSIDE COUNTY CORONER, THREE ASSISTANT CORONERS, FOUR BIOLOGY STUDENTS FROM UC-RIVERSIDE, A YOUNG WAITRESS AT THE SERRANO RESORT RESTAURANT**, and her **BUSBOY**

And now, let the mayhem begin...

PART ONE

Prelude

▶ It was a hot June night in Southern California. The full moon presided over the eerie, beautiful high desert – bathing its bizarre rocks, uncanny vegetation, and magnificent mountains in a pale blue glow.

Earlier that day, in a remote patch of the craggy wilderness, the ever-rumbling faults had cracked open a cavernous fissure. A mist of icy vapor arose from the rift. And deep within the bowels of the earth, something stirred – something unseen in the darkness – something *seething*. Ancient lungs rippled to life, and hunters reborn now crept upwards into the moonlight.

▶ A young couple, Robert Nishida and Lauri Young, had just left an impromptu engagement party thrown for them by friends. They cruised north on an old two-lane highway in Robert's open-air Jeep Wrangler – headed towards the ranch owned by Lauri's folks.

Lauri snuggled close to Robert and rested her head on his shoulder. Her blonde hair cascaded onto his chest, but her big blue eyes were wide open in worry. Having returned from college this afternoon, Lauri was supposed to have met her parents at the party – but they never arrived. The earthquake that hit earlier had taken down the phone lines and mobile relays, so there'd been no way to reach them.

For a while, Robert and Lauri rode in silence – a silence broken only by the occasional tapping of Lauri's suitcases against each other in the back seat.

Then Robert smiled and stroked his fiancée's hair. "Hey, c'mon. Where's my eternal optimist? ... I'm sure your folks are fine."

Lauri sighed. "You're right." She smiled up at Robert and softly kissed his shoulder.

Moments later, Robert steered his Jeep around the bend of a gently sloping hillside. Lauri, her head still on his shoulder, was nearly asleep.

Suddenly, Robert was startled by something ahead. "What in–? *GOOD GOD!*" He slammed the breaks, screeching the Jeep to a halt. Jolted awake, Lauri looked up.

Fifty yards before them stood a massive black beast. Side-lit by the moon and mostly in shadow, its hulk appeared as little more than shiny highlights on slick ebony. Whatever it was, the thing was clearly twice the size of the Jeep.

As Lauri gasped, Robert threw the Wrangler in reverse.

But Lauri heard an odd droning-sound coming from behind her and looked back to see a second beast closing in, moving faster than the first. "Look out! There's another!"

Robert braked again, stomped his Jeep into low gear, and headed off-road – down into the terrain.

The Jeep careened through the sand and dirt. Driving as fast as the rugged land would allow, Robert deftly steered around the scattered rocks.

Panicking, Lauri looked back. She could see the pursuing monsters, working their spindly legs in a fury to gain ground. "They're coming after us!"

Robert accelerated and, unable to dodge the smaller rocks, began taking them head-on. To avoid getting stuck in a powdery wash, Robert turned left into a small canyon. But now he faced larger rocks and had to swerve wildly, spraying sand from his tires.

Lauri stood and held the roll bar to look back at their pursuers. Robert had successfully put more distance between them.

She shouted, "What *are* these things?!"

Worried, Robert glanced at Lauri for an instant – and then *BAM!* His front right tire hit a large stone and blew, launching the Jeep upward.

Lauri was thrown clear and landed in a bed of sand. She rolled to a stop – scraped, but okay. Badly shaken, Lauri took a deep breath and stood, trying to get her bearings. She heard Robert moan and looked up to see the Jeep, resting on its left side, with Robert lying beneath.

"Robert!" She ran over and knelt beside him. "Oh, honey!"

Robert's left leg was pinned under the auto. With his arms and right leg, Robert had been trying, to no avail, to push the vehicle up enough to free himself. Wincing in pain, he looked to Lauri. "Try to tilt the Jeep!"

3

Nodding, Lauri shoved her fallen suitcases aside, rose, and gripped the roll bar. But as she strained to push upward, the first beast popped up on top of the Jeep and paused – hissing loudly! Lauri screamed and fell backwards. Robert gasped.

Terrified, the young couple stared up from the ground.

The monster had paused to look down upon the two creatures trembling beneath it, satisfied that each would make a good meal. It slowly moved downward, extending two giant claws.

Robert struggled harder to free himself.

Lauri grabbed her largest suitcase and, standing, swung it defiantly at the beast – screaming, *"No!"*

Four days earlier ...

Chapter 1

▶ Dan Montgomery could hear the growing wind and the distant thunder rumbling across the Missouri plains. The evening storm was pushing closer, and he was glad to be sheltered inside the small tented platform atop the power pole.

There was only one last cable to secure. He'd already fastened the end, but it needed a final tightening. Once that was done, Dan would reach the end of a 20-hour shift. His fit 42-year-old body was screaming for sleep, and he forcibly blinked – fighting to stay awake.

As the wind whipped the canvas, Dan could hear another truck arriving. *The supe's here to check in on me*, Dan thought, as he pulled out his thermos. Dan heard a truck door slam and then Howard Evans shouting up from below.

"Dan! Wrap it up! The storm's really close!"

"One second, and I'll have it!" Dan gulped his last ounce of coffee and moved over to the connection.

"You're well past golden time, man. I'm worried about ya."

With his large, insulated wrench, Dan secured the cable within seconds. He smiled as he gave it a tug.

"Done, Howie!" Dan shouted.

He shoved the wrench into his tool belt and flicked over its lock strap. But Dan was too tired to notice that the Velcro hadn't caught. He stepped out of the tent, letting the gaffs on his boots cut into the wooden pole, and fastened his safety harness.

After descending a few steps, Dan had to pause – head aching and mind reeling. His view of the St. Louis skyline pitched and blurred, frozen only by a flash of lighting. Dan lost his balance and began to slip. The harness broke his fall, but the jolt knocked the wrench from his belt.

Hitting the street below, the tool blew apart – one piece flying just past Howard's head. Dan recovered his senses then looked down, aghast.

There was Howard, safe, but glaring-up at him. "Lemme buy ya a Starbucks, Dan ... and we'll talk."

6

► An hour later, Dan was driving his car in the storm. He had to tell his wife, Linda, of the change of plans for the next few weeks. But Dan was grateful for it. *Bless Howie's heart! Always lookin' out for everyone, and he's right! It is time I take a break!*

The economy had royally sucked for the working man for well over three decades now. Even if you were a member of a union, they had next to no power anymore – not since organized labor had been castrated years ago. Rollbacks had taken away virtually all of the gains the locals had previously won. So, even with Dan's regular job at St. Louis Power and with Linda working full-time at the zoo, the Montgomerys had barely been making ends meet.

And with two kids – one of them having special needs – Dan also had to grab electrical repair jobs on the side. He knew the kids wondered why he wasn't around for them, and he was especially concerned about Jennie. At 16, Jennie had reached the raging-to-be-independent stage, and Dan sensed that his constantly being at work wasn't helping the matter. *Thank God, Linda's such a trooper!*

► The animal clinic at the St. Louis Zoo was a top-notch facility and Linda Montgomery, at 37, was proud to be its lead veterinarian. Every creature there sensed the love she radiated. And they were instinctively comfortable in her presence – especially the beautiful long-haired lynx that Linda was vaccinating. While Linda's gloved assistant, Kevin, safely held the cat, the creature never felt the needle and purred happily from all the attention.

Linda withdrew the syringe and rubbed the lynx between its ears. "There. You're up to date now, baby." She thanked Kevin, and he left to return the cat to its lair.

Then, as Linda was updating the records on her tablet, Dan stumbled in, looking thrashed. Startled, Linda crossed over to him. "Darling! You alright?"

Dan sighed and nodded, giving her a quick peck. "I nearly fell tonight."

"Oh, Dan!" Worried, Linda wrapped her arms around him. "You've been pushing way too hard."

"Linda ... see if we can borrow Uncle Ted's Winnebago."

"Huh?"

"That vacation time I've been saving? ... Howie says I use it now or lose it."

"Uhhh..." Linda was flustered at first, but the realization that they would all finally get to spend some time together made her brighten. "Alright," she nodded. "I can swing it."

▶ Four days later, Uncle Ted's Minnie-Winnie, with the Montgomerys stuffed inside, was cruising west along Interstate 8 in Southern Arizona, warmed by the sun rising behind them.

After passing through Tucson, Dan crowed from the driver's seat, "Hey! Take a gander at all the Saguaro cacti here! You won't see 'em after we head up into the Mojave."

"Aw, this is classic, Dad!" Patrick, Dan and Linda's 13-year-old boy, sat on his bunk in back – gazing out the window and soaking up the Sonoran Desert's beauty.

When very young, Patrick had contracted a rare illness at a less-than-efficient day care center. He'd recovered, but the disease left him mildly crippled – forcing him into a life of geekdom. Now, Patrick's constant companions were crutches, a collapsible wheelchair, and a laptop computer. But he wasn't bitter. Patrick understood how his illness had burdened the family, and he appreciated everything they'd done for him.

"A far cry from the prairies back home. Ain't this just dope, Sis?" Grinning, Patrick looked over at Jennie.

But Jennie didn't hear him. Sporting a red punk fade cut, the 16-year-old was lying on her bunk with her nose buried in the latest issue of DECIBEL – ears covered by back-of-neck headphones that blasted hard rock from a generic mp3 player. She couldn't have cared less where they were or where they were going.

Patrick, on the other hand, had his laptop in front of him. A thumb drive hand-labeled *Wikipedia* was jammed into its USB port. The boy typed *saguaro* into the search blank, tapped *enter*, and began reading.

In the front passenger seat, Linda was checking a printed road map. "I'm tellin' ya ... been misled too many times by those routing apps." She entered their destination into her smart phone and waited for Waze to calculate the route. "Okay, according to the map, it looks best to take Route 95 north to I-10, then west on 10 for quite a ways 'till we get to Whitewater, and finally 30 miles north on 18." The app finally beeped, and Linda checked the screen. "And whaddaya know? It agrees!"

Dan smiled as she placed her phone in its dash mount.

By the time they crossed into California, Linda and Dan had traded places – Linda driving, with Dan snoozing in the passenger seat. As Patrick rose from his bunk and hobbled over to the bathroom, an annoyed Jennie jerked her legs out of his path.

Jennie resented being yanked from home to waste two weeks with her fossil-minded folks and nerdy brother. Worse yet, Dan's rule of *no smartphone on the trip* cut her off from her besties. Of course, there was also the little matter of being caught, a week ago, trying to buy some Molly over Snapchat. But Jennie *had* managed to transfer her tunes onto this Chi-Fi *mPod3* player she'd swiped from Walmart. And that, she figured, would at least keep her sane.

Before too long, Dan had moved back to sleep in Jennie's bunk and Jennie was up front next to Linda. At Whitewater, Linda exited I-10 and went north onto Route 18 – a small two-lane highway. After several miles, they passed a hand-made road sign with 'San Andreas Fault' scrawled on it.

Huh, thought Linda. *If it hadn't been marked by some local, you'd 've never realized this was even it.* She turned to Jennie. "You see that, sweetie?"

But the brain-sealed teen was rocking out on an air guitar to her music. Amused, Linda failed to notice the field they'd just passed – a patch of High Desert land, littered with oil pumps and crisscrossed piping.

▶ Further back in the Richmark Oil Field, attorney Frank Stewart was wrapping up a meeting with the operations foreman in front of a trailer that served as the fracking command center. A bevy of hard-hatted Hispanic workers was scrambling in the area about them, expeditiously connecting pipes and high-pressure pumps to a well-head.

Frank handed the foreman a large manila envelope. "You've no problem. We made sure we'd be exempt from EPA regs."

The foreman took the envelope and smiled. "Still, I'll sleep better at night knowing these certificates are in our safe. Thanks."

"My pleasure. And speaking of which, I've got to be heading on."

"Well, let me see you out."

As they walked towards his RV, Frank glanced at the men scurrying about. "You work these tonks on Saturdays too?"

The foreman clucked then lowered his voice. "They make so little, they're too scared to refuse."

"Sweet."

Frank had made a killing as a principal attorney inside Richmark's New York legal department. And, at 53, Frank was driving a Class-A super coach to prove it – a large motor-home that was obscenely more luxurious than most houses. Approaching the vehicle, the foreman beamed. "Wow! What's the deal with you and *this* beast?'

"Oh, just turned the delivery of these certs into a cross-country vacation.

At that moment, Frank's wife screamed at him from inside the coach, "You done now?!"

"In a minute, dear!"

As Frank sighed, his young daughter chimed in, "Let's *go*, Daddy!"

The chuckling Foreman gave Frank a sympathetic pat on the shoulder. "I like your style."

▶ Lauri Young was checking under the hood of her disabled Mazda MX-5 and laughed into her cell phone. "Of all the places to get stuck on 18, I *would* break down on the rim of Dead Man's Pass," she said to her future father-in-law, Al Nishida, who was on the other end of the call.

The name Dead Man's Pass sounded worse than it really was. The moniker was a remnant from 65 years ago when this part of 18 was a dangerously narrow blacktop along the cliff-side. Since then, the state had blasted the upper cliff wall to significantly widen the two-lane highway. Nonetheless, Lauri was stuck there – fortunately on the inside shoulder.

Dressed in junior park ranger attire, the 23-year-old blue-eyed blonde was the very image of an athletic California Girl. She'd just obtained her degree in conservation and was returning home from college.

Lauri saw her engine problem and lifted a loose hose. "Ah, looks like a broken hose-clamp. ... Oh wait, Al!" Hearing the sound of an auto grinding up the hill, Lauri raised her head. As she stepped out to flag it down, the Montgomery's Winnebago came around the bend.

Linda stopped the RV and Jennie brightened. She yanked off the headphones and stuck her head out the window. "Need help?"

Happy to be rescued, Lauri trotted over to Jennie. "You're headed for Desert Rocks, right?"

Several minutes later, the Winnebago was trekking forward on level ground. Lauri, along with her two suitcases, found herself sitting in the back talking to Jennie and Patrick. Patrick handed her a cold diet cola.

"Thanks."

As Lauri reached for the can, Jennie couldn't help but notice her engagement ring. "Hey, nice rock!"

"Well, thank you!"

Dan was back at the wheel now, grinning as he heard Lauri giggling, and was happy that Jennie had started to open-up. While continuing north on 18, he noticed a big roll of electrical cable and a locked California-Edison truck near the roadside.

Not unusual for Saturday, Dan thought. *They'll be back, Monday.*

Chapter 2

▶ Fifteen miles later, the Waze woman robotically declared, "In one mile, turn left onto Deh-surt Rocks Roe-ad." And a minute later, Dan was doing just that.

It's not like he could've missed it, though. Two large signs at the T-junction made it quite clear that the small town of Highridge was 8 miles north on 18, that Whitewater and I-10 were 30 miles south on 18, and that Desert Rocks State Park was a mile west on Desert Rocks Road.

Shortly, Dan found himself standing outside his idling Winnebago – paused at the park's entranceway. As Dan squinted at the empty guard booth, senior park ranger Al Nishida – a spry Nisei in his late 80's – stepped out of the nearby bungalow.

"Greetings!"

Lauri bounced out of the Winnie's side door with her luggage. "Papa-san!" She ran over to Al, dropped her bags, and gave him a bear hug.

"Lauri! Glad you were rescued."

As Dan approached Al to greet him, Lauri gestured at the motor home. "Al, this is Dan Montgomery and family."

"Of course," Al said, shaking Dan's hand. "You're on our guest list. Thanks for helping."

"No problem. It was *our* pleasure."

"Well, head on in. You'll see the open campsites as you enter. Most of them have connections."

"Great," said Dan as he returned to the Winnie. "I'll let you know which one we take."

Lauri thanked Dan again. But as she reached for her suitcases, Al grabbed the largest one and nudged her toward the house. "So, how's our new graduate, anyway?"

▶ Driving into the park, the Montgomerys beheld a wondrous panorama of Joshua Trees, rock towers, and large beige boulders. Inside the central picnic grounds, four young students tossed a Frisbee back-and-forth. A neat gravel road, which circled the picnic area, sported several campsites on its perimeter. While a few tents and trailers had already claimed most of the spots, one was still open.

Dan wasted no time slipping his Winnebago into it, right next to another site that held an open screen-house. Seated on a rock in front was 11-year-old Billy Hernandez, scribbling onto a length of masking tape that he'd stuck to his model RC helicopter. He fiddled with his control unit, and the little chopper rose into the air.

As Dan killed the Winnie's engine, the tiny copter flitted up to hover outside their windshield. The strip of tape read, "Welcome to Desert Rocks!"

Dan and Linda smiled and waved at the small video camera fixed to its bottom, Linda saying, "Aw, ain't that sweet?"

But then the chopper, a miniature Apache AH-64, fired its toy machine guns – strobing LED's that synched to an audible rat-tat-tat. As Dan and Linda cracked-up, the copter did an aerial somersault and flew away.

▶ Lauri was seated in Al's living room, speaking to her mother over the land line. The weathered bungalow was decorated in a blend of Asian and Western styles, with several Japanese watercolors adorning the walls.

"No, the car's fine. Al has hose clamps in his shed, so Rob 'n I'll go back for it later." Lauri listened a moment then laughed. "Mom, you know Al hoards *everything* in that shed."

"A hopeless pack-rat, I am," said a grinning Al, as he entered from the kitchen – bearing a pitcher of iced green tea and two glasses.

"Okay, we'll see you 'n Dad here tonight. ... Love you, too. Bye." Lauri hung up then anxiously crossed to peer out the nearest front window.

Al handed her a glass of tea. "Here, with the pinch of stevia you like."

Giving Al a peck on his forehead, Lauri beamed, "Oh you're a sweetheart, thanks." She turned her head back to the window and sipped. "Rob due back soon?"

Al checked his wristwatch, "In about ten minutes."

Lauri's smile grew.

▶ Billy and Patrick had wasted no time becoming friends. As Billy showed Patrick his model copter, Dan and Linda began plugging the Winnebago into their site's electric feed. At that instant, a horn tooted, and a vintage VW Camper Van backed up to the side of the screen-house.

Billy rushed over. "Dad! Mom!"

"Yo, kiddo!" Out of the van stepped Tom Hernandez, followed by his wife, Yoli – a friendly Tex-Mex couple in their mid-30's who, being covered with crystals and colorful clothing, might very well have been taken as the world's last hippies. Tom handed Billy two bags of groceries. "Have Al plant these in his deep freeze for us, okay?"

"Right!" exclaimed Billy, running off with the bags.

Dan, Linda, and Patrick had crossed to greet Tom and Yoli. Even Jennie, curious to see what was happening, appeared at the Winnebago's door.

"*Hola!* I'm Tom Hernandez. My wife, Yoli. And it looks like you've met Billy."

Dan smiled, shaking Tom's hand. "Yeah, he's one of the family now. ... Dan Montgomery. Linda, Patrick, and uh," Dan nodded back at the Winnie, "our daughter, Jennie."

Remaining at the door, Jennie tendered a half-hearted wave.

"Hey," Tom gestured at the surrounding boulders, "your first time here?"

Linda nodded. "Sure is."

"Oh, you're gonna love it!" Yoli closed her eyes and lifted her palms as if to feel the energy. "These rocks put out the most *healing* vibes."

"Yeah," added Tom, "the Injuns called this place *the Altar of Peace*."

Dan glanced approvingly over at Linda and responded, "Ah, well, that's *just* what we need."

"Say I hope you're all hungry," chimed Yoli. "We've just come from Highridge with the fixin's for tonight's party!"

Patrick's eyes brightened. "Party?"

"Yeah, Al's boy recently got engaged," explained Tom, "so we're throwin' a little bash tonight in the couple's honor."

► Robert Nishida, at a vibrant 35, assisted his father in running the park. With a major in conservation and a minor in photojournalism, it was only natural that Robert would conduct the walking tours. And at this moment, Robert was guiding two couples – the Johnsons and the Reyeses – on a photo safari into one of the park's more exotic spaces.

Jim and Anne Johnson were an African American couple in their mid-80's. A retired postmaster from Indiana, Jim was now lolling around the country with his amiable wife in their small Silverstream trailer. Desert Rocks had long been on their bucket list, so here they were.

Michael and Elaine Reyes were on their honeymoon, modest as it may have been. But that didn't matter. The high-spirited couple were head-over-heels for each other. Born and raised in Los Angeles' historic Filipinotown, the mid-20's Michael was employed at his father's auto repair shop and was destined to take it over. Though a tad preoccupied with projecting the macho image of a Satanas gang member, Michael was, in truth, a total teddy bear – his loving nature in full swing when around Elaine. And, standing at five-foot-two, his 19-year-old bride was so beautiful it hurt. Two years prior, Elaine and her parents had migrated from their farm in the central Philippine Islands. So, in balancing her new life with the mindset of a provincial village girl, Elaine had grown into an unassuming and radiant young lady.

With Robert leading, the group strolled around a huge boulder into a breath-taking canyon. "Now, this area is called Hidden Valley. You see that big rock up ahead?" They paused. Fifty feet before them was a cracked boulder resembling the head of a troll.

"Whoa, doggy!" exclaimed Jim. "Looks like my worst nightmare!"

"We've named it the Ogre's Skull!" Robert waved everyone closer. "Your best shot's from over here."

Elaine ran ahead to pose. "Oh, Michael – take my picture!"

As Michael grabbed shots on his smartphone, Robert raised his Nikon and Jim planted his tripod, on which was mounted a vintage Stereo-Realist.

"Stay there and model for us, sweetie," shouted Anne.

"Okay!" Happy to play along, the girl draped herself over the skull's lower jaw – raising her arm and feigning a scream, like Wray being offered to Kong. "How 'bout a sacrificial virgin?"

"Oh sure," Michael laughed, "a week into our honeymoon?!!"

As everyone clucked over that one, Elaine began to turn her shoulders. "Aw! You mean I ... how do you say it? ... 'fall short of qualifying'?" And as she faced them, Elaine fell off the Ogre's jaw – hitting the ground, giggling.

Chapter 3

▶ At the Richmark oil field, the foreman, a pump operator, and the other workers were driving a series of huge pumps at the well-head – their motors whining under the strain. The foreman and the operator, Manny, were under an elevated canopy – peering intently at a laptop. The display, labeled "Deep Water Disposal", showed 30-percent progress at 50-percent pressure.

The foreman looked at his watch and started breathing down Manny's neck. "Increase the pressure by another third."

Knowing this was not a good idea, Manny hesitated. "Señor?!"

"We've pulled it off before just fine! ... *Increase the Goddamn pressure!* We don't have all day!"

Intimidated, Manny complied. The pumps howled, and the ground began to vibrate. The foreman smiled as the graphs rose to his liking.

▶ Outside their Winnebago, Patrick held up a hose – keeping it level – as Dan finished connecting it to the water feed. With the spigot's handle squeaking, Dan turned on the flow. He looked up, through the Winnie's kitchen window, at Linda. "Okay, honey. All systems go!"

Inside the RV, Linda turned on the water, and the underground pipes began to whine. Jennie, lying on her bunk, cringed at the noise. The water line continued to resonate, and the pipes outside started to shake.

In the screen-house, Tom grabbed a cold beer from his cooler and, hearing the pipes, looked over at Dan. "Aw, don't mind that. The water 'round here's awful hard."

▶ The oil field pumps were now screaming – pushed to their limit. Though the foreman was chuckling, Manny had broken into a cold sweat. As the trembling increased, the other workers stopped in their tracks, exchanging frightened glances. Something wasn't right.

"Now what are *they* stopping for?" The angry foreman jumped off his platform and strode over to the workmen, yelling, "*Hey, what the hell are–* "

Suddenly, the ground shook violently and buckled. The well-head exploded. Pipe sections, fittings, and toxic water shot everywhere. The men scrambled and fell.

At the controls, Manny killed the pumps – but the ground continued to shake. He could see the foreman stumbling towards him in shock. It wasn't until the foreman fell to the ground, dead, that Manny saw that his boss had been impaled by a fragment of pipe.

Manny jumped off the platform and stumbled over to his injured brothers. "*Juan! Jose!*"

They yelled in agony as their flesh burned from the waste raining down on them. Now drenched himself, Manny's skin blistered. He fell to the shaking ground and began to scream, his eyes burning out.

▶ At Desert Rocks, the vibrations grew stronger. There was a loud growing rumble, and the whole countryside began to quake.

Patrick gasped. "Dad! Kill the water!"

"That's not the pipes! It's an *earthquake!*" Dan lifted Patrick and dashed for the Winnie.

Headphones over her ears, Jennie fell out of her bunk. "Goddamnit, turn that off!" She managed to stand, only to see Dan and Patrick falling into the RV with Linda catching them. Trembling, Jennie turned to the window, saw the shaking desert, and screamed!

"Tom!" yelled Yoli as she and Billy dashed into their van. But Tom, still gripping his unopened beer, staggered about the screen-house, trying to keep his balance.

The rest of the campgrounds shook. The Frisbee-throwing students darted to their camps and hid in their vehicles.

Al and Lauri, who had been through quakes before, stood on Al's front porch – holding on to the support beams. But as the quake continued, Al peered into the campgrounds with concern. The boulder on top of a nearby rock tower was teetering.

Steve Lacy – a stoned 19-year-old loner – staggered out of his tent and looked about, dumbfounded. "Whoa, bad shit!" Steve threw down his joint, turned, then froze – seeing that his Harley was about to tip over.

The teetering boulder fell. Al saw this and dashed off his porch.

Unaware that a boulder was rolling straight for him, Steve gripped his bike's handlebars. In the next instant, Al's hands joined Steve's, and they yanked the bike from the boulder's path. The big rock rolled past and came to rest near the side of Al's house.

At the same time, on a mountain top three miles away, the foundation beneath the local mobile relay tower began to crack.

In Hidden Valley, Robert waved the Johnsons and Reyeses toward the center of the canyon. "Away from the rocks! Quickly! ... It'll be okay! Just sit down and ride it!" They all hit the ground and held one another.

Elsewhere, below a string of power-grid towers, a crack began to run along a large bed of basalt. The crack widened into a fissure, and half of the basalt dropped 100 feet.

Then, as gradually as it began, the quake died.

▶ Everyone at the campgrounds began to recover their wits. The four students – Mitch Davis, Kathy Smith, David Grogan, and Gary Archer – timidly showed their faces.

David and Gary were your usual 21-year-old college buddies, celebrating the end of the semester. They'd planted a couple pup tents for themselves next to Gary's beat-up cargo van and had plopped a small beer-stuffed cooler in-between.

Mitch and Kathy, both 18-year-old African Americans, were high school sweethearts – on their own summer trip before heading off to college. Mitch was the darling running back of Baldwin Hills High, now riding an athletic scholarship to universityville. And since Kathy had been the school's hottest cheerleader, it was only natural they'd end up together. So here they were, sharing a large tent – and a single sleeping bag – next to Mitch's Mustang convertible.

The four students exchanged glances, badly shaken.

The Montgomerys and Hernandezes stepped back outside. Beer-can still in hand, Tom stumbled from his screen-house to check for damage. Dan ran over to the whining water pipe and forcefully killed the feed.

Tom nodded at Dan and smiled. "I guess, uh, maybe we should find you a different hookup?"

Yoli groaned, "Ohhh, Tomás! You can *joke* after *that*?!"

But Dan and Tom *did* laugh at the irony of it. And as Tom's laugh grew into a guffaw, he proudly opened his can of beer ... which promptly sprayed him in the face.

And Jennie, upon seeing that, finally cackled.

Al and Steve remained by Steve's tent, with Steve patting Al on the shoulder. "Thanks, man."

Lauri approached to check on them. "You two alright?"

Still dazed, Steve's brain was trying to catch up. "Yeah, uh ... I, uh, just need to ... to *stand* here for a bit."

"Okay." Lauri laughed knowingly, then, noticing the students, headed over to them. "Hey! You alright over there?!"

Mitch, Kathy, David, and Gary all nodded – Gary being the first to find his voice. "I think so."

At that second, Lauri's cell phone rang. Seeing that it was her mother, she answered while walking back to the center of camp. "Mom! You all alright? ... Ranch okay?" Lauri gave a sigh of relief. "Thank God! ... Nah, we're fine."

Al had crossed to reassure the Montgomerys and Hernandezes. "Nothing to be alarmed about. We have tremors now and then."

Jennie *was* alarmed. "You call that just a *tremor*?"

"We're *okay*, darling," said Dan, trying to calm her.

Still, Jennie couldn't contain herself. "I'd hate to be in what he calls a *big* one."

Linda gave her a nudge.

But Al knew he had to prepare them. "Well, please be ready for an aftershock or two. It's likely not over."

"Oh, great!" Fed up, Jennie walked away.

Unexpectedly, a horn bellowed near the park entrance. Al glanced over and excused himself.

As Jennie strolled toward the picnic grounds, she saw Steve moving his Harley next to his tent. She paused. Steve glanced her way and smiled. And Jennie smiled back.

Chapter 4

▶ Honking repeatedly, Frank Stewart drove his super coach up to the guard booth and stopped. "Hey, who's minding the store?"

"Welcome to Desert Rocks," said Al, approaching the super coach. "May I help you?"

"Shouldn't you be here at the gate, bud?"

Al just smiled. "When not shepherding my flock."

"Okay, Moses," sniggered Frank, "You pray-up that quake to toss me off the road?"

"Wasn't easy," Al chuckled, "but seriously, you alright?"

"Swerved a bit. Didn't *really* feel it 'till we pulled over."

"Well, I'm afraid quakes can come with the territory here."

"Aw, no." Frank yelled back into the coach, "Margaret, you hear that?"

Al pulled out his reservation book. "Your name please?"

"Stewart. Frank Stewart 'n family."

Margaret Stewart – 42, a trophy-wife if there ever was one – joined Frank. "What, honey?"

"You went 'n picked *Earthquake Central!* "

Margaret laughed. "So sue me, counselor." She gave Frank a quick peck and returned to the depths of their RV.

Frank shook his head and fanned his hands open, feigning exasperation.

Al closed his book. "Hey, ya know, I don't seem to have you on our reservation list."

"List? *What* list?!"

"Oh, no worry. There's plenty of space."

▶ Walking from the students' camps toward the picnic grounds, Lauri finished her phone call. "Okay, mom. See you in a bit." She slapped her cell phone into her belt and, on looking up, grew overjoyed and dashed forward. "Robert!"

Robert, followed by the Johnsons and Reyeses, had just stepped out from a trail behind the Hernandez' camp. Instantly, Lauri and

21

Robert melted into each other's arms – Robert whispering, "I have *so* missed you."

Smiling at the lovebirds, the Johnsons and Reyeses crossed toward Tom and Dan.

Tom, still toweling beer from his face, stepped over to greet them. "Hey! Glad to see you're all in one piece."

At that moment, Frank's super coach revved forward, and everyone lifted their heads to gawk at the mansion on wheels. Tom whistled, and Anne's jaw dropped.

Jim's eyes nearly popped out of his head. "Whoa, doggy!"

Frank drove the super coach around the picnic area – craning his neck, frustrated. "Damn! The good spots 'r already taken!"

As the coach turned, the Stewart's four-year-old daughter, Tiffani, stared out the back window – scowling at everyone they passed while hugging a toy doll that had clearly been custom-made to look just like her.

▶ Frank steered the super coach away, turned behind a large boulder, and pulled into a site with no other campers nearby. "Perfect!"

However, Tiffani – sitting on the rear bed and still gazing out the back window – pointed to a nicer, shaded site. "But Daddy, it's better over there!"

Frank rose and headed for the side door. "No, Tiffani. We're camping right here!" He and Margaret exited the RV, leaving their daughter to pout.

Frank and Margaret began to connect the hookups, with Margaret pulling out the water hose and Frank checking the electrical box. Scowling, Tiffani came to the door to watch.

Frank gritted his teeth. The cover plate on the outlet was barely attached, with worn wires exposed. "Look here, Margaret!"

Margaret crossed to peer over his shoulder.

"This," growled Frank, as he cautiously pulled the wires out a bit, "is a negligence suit waiting to happen!"

Margaret turned to Tiffani. "Oh honey, can you fetch the little screwdriver for Daddy?"

"*NO!*" Tiffani yanked the door shut so hard that it startled Frank into crossing the bare wires – the sparks jolting him!

Fuming, Frank stood. "I'll flippin' kill her!" He strode to the door.

And Margaret was right on his tail. "Frank!"

Frank reached for the door knob. Locked! Margaret giggled, infuriating Frank even more. He yanked out his keys, opened the door, and roared in. "Don't you *ever* talk to your mother like that!"

But as Margaret joined in, an aftershock hit – a huge one! The super coach rocked wildly.

Inside, Tiffani shrieked. Frank teetered. Margaret grabbed Tiffani. Frank grabbed them both. And they all hung on for dear life.

▶ This time, the campgrounds rolled in long waves. Most everyone stumbled to their vehicles. Seeing the beers bouncing out of their cooler, David and Gary held down its lid – riding the ground waves like a bounding bronco.

Back at the mobile relay tower, the cracked foundation ruptured, and the tower toppled.

At the basalt fissure, the sunken half fell *another* 100 feet – exposing a wall of quartz. Like lightning, cracks shot through the crystal, and the wall shattered inward. Hot desert air rushed in, quenching a vacuum that hadn't been filled in eons. Dust and ice particles flew everywhere, and the aftershock subsided.

A massive underground cavern had just been unsealed. And deep within the cavern's darkness, beneath its ancient icy dust, something monstrous slept – a horror frozen since the beginning of time.

▶ Together, Al and Robert walked through the campgrounds – Al shouting, "Everyone alright?!"

The campers genially waved and answered back, having weathered this one much better. The students pulled beers from the cooler for themselves, and Jim stepped out from his Silverstream.

Frank popped up between a couple of boulders. "Hey, ranger! The damned 'lectric hookup over here nearly killed me. Now it doesn't even have juice!"

Al paused. "Aw-oh."

23

"We didn't fix 13 yet." Robert shook his head and walked on.
Jim Johnson hailed Al as well. "Al, *our* power's out."

"Yeah, ours too," yelped Michael as he and Elaine approached.

"Okay, I'm really sorry, folks," Al sighed as he crossed toward
Frank. "But until Cal-Ed gets us back on, we'll just have to use
our generators."

"Assuming we even *have* generators!" Michael fumed.

Elaine gently patted Michael's shoulder and whispered, "Then
we'll make do with candlelight." She flicked her tongue in his ear
and, instantly, Michael was jello.

As Robert stepped onto Al's porch, Lauri came out of the front
door. "Rob, I can't reach Mom 'n Dad."

"Huh?"

"Landlines are out," she raised her cell phone, "and I can't get a
signal now."

"Probably just blown relays."

"Look, I know you guys don't want to say it in front of our
guests, but those weren't our *average* little tremors."

"Don't worry." Robert gave her a hug. "Your folks 'll be here
soon. ... Tell you what. ... If you don't mind pulling 'round my
Jeep, I'll raid the shed for clamps and water, and we'll go fetch
your car." He raised his key ring. "Deal?"

"Deal," Lauri grabbed the keys and kissed him.

▶ Ken and Joyce Young were cattle ranchers, owning a small but
profitable spread eight miles north of Desert Rocks, off 18 – just a
half-mile past the Sand Canyon bridge. Practical, hard-working
canyon folk in their mid-40's, the Youngs were thrilled over their
daughter returning from college today.

While Ken was outside inspecting their barn for damage, Joyce
was in the living room, trying to phone Lauri.

Ken returned through the front door. "Things look fine, honey.
If there's any damage, it's only the cattle gettin' a touch spooked.
And they're *already* brushin' it off." He grinned at Joyce. "You
reach our little girl again?"

Joyce shook her head, worried. "There's no service on the
landline *or* the mobiles now."

"Aw, only natural things 'd be down." Ken gave her a hug.
"She'll be fine."

24

Smiling, her head on his chest, Joyce tugged at Ken's dusty shirt. "Hey, you clean up while I change." She nudged him towards their bedroom. "We'll have to head over soon enough."

Ken and Joyce made a handsome couple, and Joyce looked much younger than her years. If you'd bumped into her and Lauri out shopping together, you might have taken them for sisters rather than mother and daughter.

▶ At the fissure, mist rose from the cavern opening – primeval moisture diffusing into the present-day heat.

The monstrosity in the depths of the cavern, warmed by the desert's dry breath, had nearly thawed. Gradually, its primal lungs began to ripple, and the beast's cold blue-green blood sluggishly pulsed through its body. A pair of giant black claws slowly rose from the stone floor. And, as its consciousness returned, the beast sensed it was awakening from a *very* long sleep. This was the male Bull – the king of his clan.

In a rising whisper, a consonance of many rippling book-lungs multiplied throughout the caverns around him. The entire nest had just revived, as well.

Chapter 5

▶ On the edge of Desert Rocks' picnic area, Tom had assembled an open metal kitchenette next to the permanent grills. He took his barbequing seriously and was happily basting a pile of steaks with his secret beer and brown sugar marinade. Linda, Yoli, Michael, Elaine, Jim, and Anne arrived to help set things up.

Michael dumped coals into the grills, and Elaine shot them with starter fluid.

With a long match, Jim set the grills ablaze, facetiously chanting, "May this flame appease the Earth God and quiet his rage."

"Amen to that," laughed Michael, as the three raised their beers in a toast.

"*Siya nawa!*" responded Elaine, who turned to Jim and giggled. "You just prayed to *Panlinugun.*"

"Huh?" inquired Jim.

"Her island's folklore," explained Michael.

"*O-o,*" nodded the girl. "Panlinugun is the god of earthquakes, and..." suddenly, Elaine began to shiver, "...legend says that when he shakes the earth, *Sidapa* follows in his wake."

"Sidapa?" asked Jim.

Elaine clutched the gold cross hanging from her neck. "The goddess of death."

Sensing his wife's fear, Michael hugged her. "Hey, sweetheart! Didn't your priests ban all that long ago?"

Her head on his chest, Elaine smiled. "You were born here, my love. But I'm from Samar." She looked into his eyes. "And we Visayans worshipped the Diwata for a thousand years before Spain's priests arrived. But...yes...we now have Jesus to protect us. Don't we?"

Elaine devoutly raised her cross and kissed it. Though, with her mind dredging up the legends her grandma secretly taught her years before, Elaine did her best to suppress a sense of dread.

"Okay, let's lighten the mood here." Docking his smart phone into his boom-box, Michael punched up a catchy Fil-Pop dance tune. As they worked, everyone began moving to the music.

▶ Dan had gone to Al's storage shed to retrieve the last bag of Tom's steaks from the freezer. The shed was kept fairly cool by the shade of two fan palms and an old Sears swamp-cooler that Al had jammed into a window.

After removing the bag, Dan turned and paused a moment to survey the shed's contents – plenty of canned food, gasoline canisters, Sterno, kerosene, pesticides, several shotguns, ammo, fence stakes, and large bails of chicken wire. There was a small workbench with tools and respirators, and even a washer and dryer. Heading to the door, Dan chuckled to himself. *If his folks lived through the Depression, Al caught the hoarding bug from them. ... He could survive a zombie apocalypse with all this!*

On exiting the shed, Dan saw that Al was nearby, stooped next to an old generator. He had removed its side panel and was unfastening the interior coil. "Damn!"

What's the matter?" asked Dan as he approached.

Al rose with the coil in his hand, growling, "Awh, my moldy old generator. Look!" As he raised the coil, it disintegrated in the gentle grip of his fingers, crumbing into copper dust.

Dan politely stifled a laugh. "'fraid that's beyond hope, Al." To avoid being asked to tackle an impossible repair, Dan started to back away. "Uhm, maybe one of the campers 'd be willing to lend you *theirs*."

Brushing his hands, Al belted out a sarcastic laugh. "You know *that* ain't in the cards!" As Dan strode back to the picnic grounds, Al looked down at the motor, sighed, and gave it a swift kick. The entire unit collapsed.

▶ Robert and Lauri were in Robert's Jeep Wrangler, headed east on Desert Rocks Road. Arriving at the T-junction with 18, they turned right and headed south.

▶ Dan plopped the steaks next to Tom and crossed to help Linda, Yoli, and Steve move four picnic tables into a long single line.

Even the Stewarts joined the proceedings. While Frank and Tiffani sat down to watch everyone else work, Margaret pasted on a smile and crossed to help Yoli and Elaine set the tables.

Across from the picnic area, the Montgomery's portable generator was feeding juice to the Winnebago.

Inside, Jenny was lying on her bunk, reading her magazine. Headphones over her ears, she'd cranked up some hard rock on her mPod3 to drown out Michaels' boom-box. But right then, Jennie heard a quick *scrub*, and her music ceased. "What the–?"

Annoyed, she fiddled with the cheap player's buttons. Its tiny LCD screen displayed a flashing *unhappy pod-face* and read *corrupted files – reformat memory.*

"No way!" Jennie stepped through the menus, nearly in tears. Then, she brightened.

The display now read *AM/FM Tuner*, and Jennie hit *scan*. The radio moved through a few staticky stations – pausing briefly on an echoing Spanish talk show, Mexican oomp-pah-pah, and then a shrieking Mariachi band.

Her head about to explode, Jennie happened upon a news bulletin. *"...the KXKI newsroom, here's more regarding the quakes which have rocked Southern California today."*

Abruptly, Jennie sat up, adjusting her headphones.

"Reports of severe damage are now coming in from San Bernardino and neighboring communities."

Jennie flew to the front of the RV where Patrick and Billy were sitting next to the laptop, intently playing a video game. "Patrick?!"

"Nah now, sis!"

"Several buildings are reported to have collapsed in addition to the Interstate 10 overpass near Bingham Avenue."

Frustrated, Jennie shot out the door and dashed towards the picnic area – passing Linda, who saw her alarm.

"Jennie?"

"It *was* a bad one!"

Arriving at Michael's boom-box, Jennie swapped Michael's phone with her player.

"Hey!" exclaimed Tiffani when the music shut off.

Now everyone paused, lending an ear to the report.

"...is believed there are substantial fatalities, though it's too early to determine any number. The San Bernardino Fire Department has stated that hundreds of people could lie buried beneath the rubble. Therefore, all rescue units from San Bernardino, Riverside, and Los Angeles Counties have been directed to the disaster area."

Drawn by the radio, Al and the students joined the group. Margaret moved back over to Frank and pulled Tiffani close to her.

"Fortunately, it appears that the rest of the Southland has not experienced anything beyond minor damage and scattered power outages."

Distressed by the newscast, Yoli and Elaine nervously resumed setting the tables.

"This just in to our newsroom. CalTech has determined that the epicenter of the quake lies about twenty miles north of San Bernardino – roughly halfway between Apple Valley and Arrowhead."

A look of shock fell across Frank's face, and he whispered to himself, "No ... can't be!"

"This is Buddy Maxwell reporting. Please stand by for more..."

Michael yanked the player from his boom-box. "Enough! But thank you." He handed the player to Jennie.

Margaret asked Frank, "Didn't we drive through there today?"

Frank nodded silently, the quake's likely cause hitting him.

Michael turned to Al. "Anyone here from San Berdoo?"

Al shook his head. "Everyone's either from LA or out of state."

Growing pale, Frank pulled out his iPhone and mumbled, "It just can't be. ... Oh shit!" He saw that his phone had no signal.

"Come on, everybody!" rallied Tom. "Don't be down. It's not like there's anything we can do about it. ... And besides, there's our newly-engaged couple we're celebrating tonight!"

Michael fist-pumped, "Hell, yes!" He then looked around – realizing that Robert and Lauri weren't there – and laughed. "Uh ... hey, where are they?"

"Down 18, retrieving Lauri's car," answered Al. "They'll be back shortly."

▶ Snuggled together, Robert and Lauri rode in the open-air Wrangler. Though nearly sunset, the air was still hot – and so were they.

"You know," purred Lauri, as she stroked Robert between his legs, "it's all I can do keep from tearing your clothes off and eating you alive."

Robert felt himself hardening. "Frankly, my dear, the feeling's mutual." He playfully snapped his teeth at her.

Lauri sighed and paused, partly crying and laughing. "If only we didn't have a camp full of people waiting for us."

"Later," Robert smiled, "*after* the party."

As Robert kissed Lauri's forehead, they drove past the locked Cal-Ed truck and the big role of cable that Dan had spotted on his way in.

▶ Inside the cavern, the Bull male was nearly revived and beginning to sense light again. The eyes fixed on top of his head looked like a pair of crystal balls. Separated by five inches, they endowed the beast with sweeping stereoscopic vision. Below the main eyes and right above his oral cavity, the creature possessed six smaller eyes – three on each side – that widened his view to the ground. Though simple lenses, the Bull's eyes had evolved for night hunting and were extremely sensitive to light. Nothing in motion would escape his sight.

Hunger gnawed at the Bull's guts. And he knew that if he was hungry, the others in his nest were too. The monster rose on long jointed legs, ready to fulfill his mission of leading the scouts in a hunt.

He began to signal them with a low droning sound – a droning so deep you'd have felt it in the pit of your stomach – a droning that declared it was time to stalk prey, to feed, and to return with scraps for the others. Gradually, the droning grew louder and multiplied into a deafening chorus. The scouts were affirming their readiness.

▶ As Robert and Lauri neared Dead Man's Pass, Robert's smile faded. "Oh, no!"

A massive rockslide had covered the highway with huge boulders, totally blocking it. Robert slowed his Wrangler to a stop, right next to Lauri's crushed and buried Mazda.

Gripping the Wrangler's roll-bar, Lauri stood and gasped. "My poor car!"

Chapter 6

▶ It was now dark. The rising full moon backlit the grid towers that rose above the fissure, lacing the cavern opening in a web of cable shadows. The droning continued from deep inside.

Now able to see clearly, the Bull moved toward the light – his scouts dutifully following. As he approached the cavern opening, the Bull instinctively recognized the moon. But the world seemed different to him, and the moon was smaller now – much smaller than before.

The beasts crept out into the desert. While most of the scouts followed the Bull, others knew it was their job to branch off and forage in other areas.

▶ "Good heavens!" exclaimed Linda. "You mean the way we came in this afternoon?!"

"Yep, right where you found me," Lauri said, scooping potato salad onto her paper plate. "We'd need a bulldozer to even make a dent."

"And with the cliff-side there, you can't exactly drive around it," added Robert.

The party had just started, and everyone was seated on the line of picnic tables, spooning up the side dishes as Tom and Yoli individually delivered their steaks.

"Wait'll ya taste *this*," vouched a beaming Tom.

After returning, the two guests of honor had promptly changed into casual wear. Robert wore beige cargo shorts, sneakers, and an open blue Aloha shirt. But Lauri – now sporting short denim cutoffs, a swimsuit top with pearl solitaire necklace, and heeled sandals – had dressed to make sure Robert's hormones would be surging. In fact, many of the others had changed into colorful summer wear too. It was a hot June night in the Mojave Desert, and ample skin was on display.

The news of the rock-slide didn't sit well with Frank. "But I've got to get to my LA office on Monday, now!"

"What?!" cried Margaret.

"An emergency's come up, dear."

This was the first Margaret had heard of it, and she was pissed.

Frank turned back to Robert and Lauri. "There isn't another route outta here?"

Lauri nodded. "Sure. Go north on 18, over the Sand Canyon Bridge, to Highridge. Then take 247 west to 14."

"But you'll be winding over mountains, so add an extra hour or two," advised Robert.

Jim snickered. "With *his* outsized coach? Better add *three or four* hours!"

Enjoying Frank's dismay, the rest of the campers chuckled.

Al changed the subject. "Lauri, I feel bad for starting without your folks."

"Have you *ever* known them to be on time? giggled Lauri. "Hey, Tom! Save some grub for 'em. They'll be here soon!"

"You got it, sweetie!"

Lauri turned to Robert. "Besides, I know what they're up to."

"Oh, yeah?"

"Saturday's their *date night*, if ya know what I mean," she whispered while stroking his thigh under the table.

Robert responded with a devilish grin and hugged her.

▶ The Bull led his followers through the desert. Not having what we know as ears and noses, the beasts could sense sound and odors through a comb-like organ on their undersides. And now the Bull both *heard* and *smelled* a creature approaching. He paused upon seeing the animal – one that was new to him.

An old starving coyote had stumbled into the Bull's path. On catching sight of the beast, the canine froze. She had no idea what freakish things her eyes beheld, but she yowled in fear and fled back the way she came.

The Bull raised a pincher and droned at his scouts to ignore her. He continued forward – leading the pack down into a sandy canyon then up and over a ridge. He sensed a flock of prey that lay ahead.

▶ The party continued in the picnic area. With the main course finished, the tables had been returned to their original positions.

The rest of the adults had either broken into groups or stood about mingling, desserts or beverages in hand. And the students had retreated to an adjacent space to toss their Frisbee.

Jim, Patrick, Billy, and Anne sat at one table playing a board game – a Luxury edition of CLUE. Tiffany stood beside Billy to watch him play and to learn the game. And with Billy being the youngest one there besides herself, Tiffani was beginning to feel the pangs of her first crush.

▶ By candlelight, Ken and Joyce had just finished dressing and were about to leave for Desert Rocks.

Joyce quipped, "Hope they hold us some grub."

"Well, we'd a been long gone if you hadn't ambushed me in the shower for a quickie."

Joyce feigned surprise. "Why, Kenneth Young! Are you *complaining*?!"

"Ha-ha, not in the least, gorgeous." Ken drew Joyce closer.

As they passionately kissed, a frightening clamor erupted outside. Their cattle began wailing – the young heifers, especially, shrieking! And mixed in was a deep droning sound, the likes of which no human had ever heard.

Ken and Joyce froze, not knowing what to make of it.

"Jeezus Christ!" Ken strode to the front room, Joyce on his tail. "The cattle!" Stopping at his gun rack, he pulled down a rifle and shotgun.

Joyce grabbed a rifle, too. "I'm goin' with you!"

"No, you're *not*! Could be cougars. So you just stay here 'till I find out what's hap'nin. ... If I need help, I'll yell." He crossed to the front door. "'n if I do, *then* you come out guns-a-blazin'!" Ken took a deep breath and dashed out into the darkness.

Joyce shut the door behind him. And as the melee grew louder, she wrung her hands.

▶ Tiffani remained by Billy and those playing CLUE. "So, can I play yet?

Billy smirked, "You sure, now, you know how?"

Having her fill of being doubted, Tiffani scowled, grabbed the *candlestick* from the game board, and ran off.

34

"Hey, bring that back!" giggled Billy, who chased after her – leaving Patrick, Jim, and Anne to crack up.

Tiffani dashed over to an arguing Frank and Margaret to show them the token. "Look, Mommy. Professor Plum did it in the library with this!"

At once, Margaret's face morphed from scowl to smile. "Oh, that's nice, sweetie. But you take that right back to where you got it, okay?"

"And don't swipe other people's stuff!" bellowed Frank.

Tiffani turned up her nose and, as Billy approached, handed the piece back to him.

"It's okay, Mr. Stewart," Billy offered. "She just wants to play with us. C'mon, Tiff." Billy put his hand on the little girl's shoulder and started walking her back to their table. "We'll start a new round and deal you in."

Margaret resumed glaring at Frank. "What fucking *emergency*, dammit?!"

"I've told you, I can't say a word 'till we've appraised things at the office. But it's really serious. Could devastate us."

"*What* could?!"

Frank just stared back at her. If she was too dense to put it together, he wasn't about to explain. Instead, Frank polished off the last few ounces from a flask of Dewar's, right in her face. Then, without a word, he rose and crossed to the Hernandez' huge, long Igloo cooler.

Rummaging through the available beers, Frank was unable to find what he deemed a worthy brew. He muttered, "This crap all they got? Can't fuckin' believe this day!"

Elaine came up and knelt beside him, pulling out two bottles of Red Horse that she'd previously buried in a corner under the ice. "Having a good time, Frank?"

Frank looked up to get a face full of cleavage and grinned lecherously. "I am *now*, baby!"

Embarrassed, Elaine smiled uncomfortably and decorously backed away.

As she returned to Michael, Frank's eyes hungrily traced up her slim brown calves and satin thighs to focus on her tight round booty.

Michael saw Frank leering as Elaine approached, but he just smiled. "Thank you, darling." He took the beer and pulled Elaine close to him, slyly glancing at Frank from the corner of his eye. *Eat your heart out, you wealthy wanker!*

Al, Dan, Linda, Tom, and Yoli were conversing at a picnic table. Tom rose to fetch more beers, and Dan turned to chat with Al. While listening and nodding, Dan momentarily glanced aside to notice Jennie and Steve talking together. They seemed to be hitting it off. But it looked innocent enough, so Dan returned his attention to Al.

Robert, Lauri, Michael, and Elaine were grouped at their own table – laughing and having a good time. But Lauri had been steadily growing nervous, and a sudden chill now shot up her spine. Worried, she glanced down at her watch. *Mom and Dad are way overdue.*

▶ As the frenzy outside continued, Joyce remained in the living room with her back against the wall.

She had heard Ken firing his rifle and shotgun multiple times. *Why hasn't he called for help?!*

The droning began to overwhelm the bleating of the cattle. Ken fired several times more, then he stopped. *Has he run out of shells?* Now, the droning grew deafening.

Ken shouted, "No! NO!" and let loose a bloodcurdling scream!

Enough! Rifle in hand, Joyce flew out the door and into the night. "Ken! Ken!"

She frantically rounded the barn then stopped dead in her tracks, facing their corral. Petrified, as if in a nightmare, Joyce could barely make sense of what she saw.

Black creatures, barely discernible against the night sky, were crawling all over the cattle.

Not cougars, thought Joyce, *but monstrous...giant...BUGS!* There were many. And scattered beneath their long legs lay the dismembered remains of the cattle and, as Joyce finally saw, of her husband!

"KEN!" cried Joyce as she stumbled forward – numbed with shock. But she froze the moment she realized that, right in front of her, Ken's limbs were being devoured by three of the monsters.

Now, several of the creatures caught sight of Joyce and paused. In front of the others, a somewhat larger bug moved a forearm in her direction – and those not feeding advanced. Joyce's adrenaline surged. She wasted no time in rapid-firing her rifle. But the bullets had no effect, and the beasts closed in.

Joyce fled for the house, hoping to barricade herself inside.

She neared the front porch.

Up the steps.

Almost through the open door, then...

SEIZED, and yanked back!

Screaming, Joyce struggled as she was viced in the grip of a huge pincher. Her ribs were crushed into her lungs. And, as she was dragged off the porch, Joyce wailed – choking on her own blood.

▶ Lauri shuddered again, turning pale, and lifted her smartphone to read the screen. Still no signal. She excused herself from Robert and the Reyeses and hurried over to Al's bungalow.

Lauri lifted Al's telephone – *dead static* – tapped the switch-hook several times – *nothing* – then replaced the receiver.

▶ A short distance from the picnic area, out of everyone's view, Jennie and Steve had hidden themselves behind a pile of large rocks. Seated on the ground, they shared a blunt – laughing – their smiling eyes now bloodshot.

"So what's with this *vacation with mommy 'n daddy* business?" asked Steve.

"Think I had any choice? Cut me some slack, will you?"

"You cut loose from them, you can have all the choices you want. Bet daddy does nothin' but hassle you, right?"

"It's not that," sighed Jennie. "Dad just has to work all the time, so he isn't around much. ... But, when he is, Polio Pat gets all the attention."

▶ Seated together, Dan and Al continued their conversation.

"Growing-up second generation, I didn't know if I was American or Japanese," related Al. "But when the war broke out, that question was answered for me."

Dan was absorbing a page of history he'd never really thought much about. "You were interned?"

Al nodded. "I was five years old."

"But that would make you..."

Al put a finger to his lips in a silent *Shhhhhh!*

"Oh, my lips are sealed, " smiled Dan, "that is, as long as you share your fountain-of-youth with me."

As the two men laughed, Lauri approached. "S'cuse me, Dan." She took Al by the hand. "Gotta borrow Papa-San for a minute."

While being dragged away, Al turned to Dan and winked, "The Okinawa diet, Dan!"

A few steps later, Lauri gravely whispered, "Al, I'm losing it. My folks are *way* overdue."

Smiling, Dan watched Al and Lauri head off. Then, he turned to discover that Jennie and Steve were gone. Dan dropped his smile and, now concerned, craned his neck around to find them. But they were nowhere to be seen.

▶ Lauri and Al stood in front of the bungalow – Lauri detailing her worries, "...and the phones are still out. Something's wrong."

"Well, they may need help then." Al pulled out his car keys. "Did they call following the aftershock?"

Lauri shook her head, holding back tears. "The phones were all out by then."

"Okay, I'll head over and see."

Robert stepped out of the house with Lauri's two suitcases. "Nah, Dad. We're going." He crossed to his Jeep and planted the luggage in back.

"Yeah," agreed Lauri. "I should be there. And Rob *has* to take me home sometime."

"You sure?" Al questioned.

"Stay here and enjoy yourself." Lauri gave Al a quick peck and crossed to the Wrangler, which Robert started.

"Well, drive slow," said Al. And as they headed away, he shouted, "We've not checked 18 north of here!"

Robert waved and yelled, "Fill you in when I get back!"

A minute later, Robert and Lauri reached the T-junction and turned left onto 18 – heading north towards Highridge.

► Sharing another blunt, Steve and Jennie were still seated in back of their snug rock pile – stoned and having a jolly time.

But at that moment, Dan walked around the corner. "Jennie?" He strode toward his daughter as she struggled to hide the blunt.

"Uh, hi Dad!"

"*Busted*," sung Steve.

In truth, Dan was relieved to see that this was all they were up to. But he still had to discourage Jennie from it. "Sweetheart, smoking's prohibited here because of the fire hazard." He bent down and took the blunt from her. "And uh, pot's still not totally legal back home, either."

Jennie cracked an innocent *you-caught-me* grin and giggled, "But we're not back home, are we?"

Dan examined the blunt and addressed Steve. "Hmm. Hemp leaf on the outside instead of tobacco. I'm impressed ... but ..." Dan dropped the blunt and crushed it under his foot.

Steve gasped.

Then Dan glared at Jennie, dead serious. "Get your butt back to our camper. You're grounded."

Crushed, Jennie rose. "Can't I just, for once, live my own life?"

"At only sixteen?" he shook his head, "*Unh*-ah!"

Linda appeared behind Dan and paused, taking in the scene. Dan stood-up.

Steve rose too, barely able to keep his balance. "You don't have to do what he says!"

Dan barked at his daughter, "Get back there, now!"

Sulking, Jennie headed for Linda, who escorted her away.

Dan turned back to Steve and placed a hand on his shoulder. "Listen, pal."

His mind clouded, Steve responded with lizard-brain reflex, "Hey man," and tried to pull his knife!

In that instant, Dan grabbed Steve's wrists, kicked his feet out from under him, and pinned him to the ground – laughing the whole time.

"Ow!"

"You stoned little punk!" Dan said, knocking Steve's knife from his hand. "As a minor, my daughter certainly *does* have to do what I say! ... Now look ... I see you're a bit out-of-it, okay?" He slowly released his grip on the boy and grabbed the knife. "So I'll forget your little macho stunt here." Dan gently put his hand on Steve's shoulder, "And you ... you'll agree to can the drugs and stay away from her."

Steve remained still and gawked up at Dan, who handed his knife back to him, handle first.

"Got it?"

Bleary-eyed, the boy accepted the blade. And, as Dan walked away, Steve dumbly stared outward. Then, his mind caught up.

"Aw, shit!" Steve stabbed his knife into the ground and buried his face in his hands, embarrassed over his own behavior.

Chapter 7

► Robert and Lauri cruised north in the Wrangler, quite alone on Highway 18. With the rockslide to the south, there were no other cars to be seen at all – not even one coming from the north.

Lauri snuggled close to Robert and rested her head on his shoulder. For a while, they rode in silence – the only odd sound being the occasional tapping of Lauri's suitcases against each other in the back seat. Lauri's eyes were wide open. She was worried sick.

Robert took note and stroked her hair. "Hey, c'mon. Where's my eternal optimist? I'm sure your folks are fine."

Lauri sighed. "You're right. It's just ... I've had the most sinking feeling for the last hour. Don't really know why."

"Well, I think you've had a *very* long day, and you're tired. Look, with that rolling aftershock, they're likely dealing with a downed fence."

Lauri smiled up at Robert. "Sorry I'm such a killjoy tonight. I'll make it up to you tomorrow."

Robert chuckled. "No rush, no problem. ... We've a whole lifetime ahead of us."

Lauri softly kissed his shoulder.

► Two of the Bull's independent scouts were aggressively searching for prey through the nearby desert. They had yet to encounter anything large enough to bother stalking, but they were famished and not about to give up.

► As the party started to wind down, Jim and Anne were the first to leave, followed by the students and Michael and Elaine. Dan, Linda, and Patrick remained to help Tom, Yoli, Billy, and Al clean the grills.

Inside the Winnebago, Jennie faked a lump in her bunk with pillows and a sleeping bag. She pulled the covers up over them, admiring her convincing handiwork.

Cautiously, Jennie opened the side door and stuck her head out to look around. She saw that Dan and Linda had their backs to her. So she quietly stepped out and snuck around to the other side of the RV. Waiting for her there, with a sleeping bag hung over his shoulder, was Steve. Jennie greeted him with a kiss, and the pair ambled away, disappearing into the boulders.

After saying goodnight, Linda and Patrick retreated to the Winnie. Dan remained to help Tom and Yoli pack the utensils.

Al shook hands with Dan and Tom, gave Yoli a hug, and then wearily shuffled towards his house.

Just beyond the picnic area, Margaret propped up an inebriated Frank as he staggered back to their super coach. Even Tiffani helped to brace him when he stumbled.

Mumbling, Frank was barely intelligible. "Lie-a-bill-tee, Marg-ret! You...dun..gettit? They...prove...it...wipe us out!"

"*What* is wrong, Frank?"

"Rich-macch syyt. Da quaykes."

Almost crying, Margaret sighed – shaking her head at the man she once thought she loved. "Frank, ... you're daft."

Al stepped onto his porch and stretched. He sat down in a plastic recliner, leaning back into its foam cushion, to wait for Robert.

Relaxing, he looked out at Desert Rocks.

It was so serene and – with everyone quietly settling into their camps, the beautiful round boulders and Joshua trees dotted about, the stars scattered above, and the full moon shining down – the vista that Al took in was magnificent.

He took a deep breath and smiled.

▶ On Route 18, Robert steered his Jeep around the bend of a gently sloping hillside. Lauri, her head still on Robert's shoulder, had nearly fallen asleep.

Just then, Robert was startled by something ahead. "What in–? *GOOD GOD!*" He slammed the breaks, screeching the Jeep to a halt. Jolted awake, Lauri looked forward.

One of the scouts had crawled up onto the highway. It believed that it was staring at another animal that had been approaching – one with two glowing eyes. Blinded by the headlights, the scout froze.

Robert and Lauri gasped. Fifty yards before them stood what appeared to be a huge repulsive bug – a monster twice as big as their Jeep.

The scout's eyes began to adjust, and it started creeping forward.

Finally catching her breath, Lauri shrieked. Robert threw the Wrangler in reverse, but Lauri heard a droning from behind and looked back. The second scout was closing in – moving faster than the first. "Look out! There's another!"

As the first scout droned in response to the second, Robert braked again. Then, he stomped his Jeep into low gear and headed off-road – down into the terrain.

The Jeep careened through the sand and dirt. Driving as fast as the rugged land would allow, Robert deftly steered around the scattered rocks.

Panicking, Lauri looked back. She could see the pursuing bugs, working their spindly legs in a fury to gain ground. "They're coming after us!"

Robert accelerated and, unable to dodge the smaller rocks, began taking them on. To avoid getting stuck in a powdery wash, Robert turned left into a small canyon. But now, he encountered larger rocks and had to swerve wildly – spraying sand from his tires. "I've hiked through here! There's a gorge ahead we can hide in!"

"Go for it!" Lauri stood and held the roll bar. She looked back at their pursuers. While Robert had successfully put more distance between them, Lauri saw each bug raise two hideous pinchers and stretch them forward – as if they could reach across infinity and seize her.

Lauri shouted, "What *are* these things?!"

Worried, Robert glanced at Lauri for an instant – and then *BAM!* His front right tire hit a large stone and blew, launching the Jeep upward.

Lauri was thrown clear and landed in a bed of sand. She rolled to a stop – scraped, but okay. Badly shaken, Lauri took a deep breath and stood, trying to get her bearings. She heard Robert moan and looked up to see the Jeep, resting on its left side, with Robert lying beneath.

"Robert!" She ran over and knelt beside him. "Oh, honey!"

Robert's left leg was not only pinned under the auto, it was broken just below the knee – gashed open and oozing blood.

With his arms and right leg, Robert had been trying, to no avail, to push the vehicle up enough to free himself. Wincing in pain, he looked to Lauri. "Try to tilt the Jeep!"

Nodding, Lauri shoved her fallen suitcases aside, rose, and gripped the roll bar. But as she strained to push upward, the first scout popped up on top of the Jeep and paused – loudly *hissing!* Lauri screamed and fell backwards. Robert gasped.

The young couple stared up from the ground, aghast! Backlit by the moon, the hideous beast was clearly visible – eight legs, eight eyes, two large pinchers, and a long segmented tail ending in a venomous stinger. No question, now, of what these monsters were. Robert and Lauri knew they were facing a *black 12-foot scorpion* – nature's most vicious eating machine, enlarged fifty fold!

The monster had paused to look upon the two creatures trembling below, satisfied that each would make a good meal. It smelled the blood from Robert's wound and slowly started to move downward.

Robert struggled even harder to free himself.

Lauri grabbed her largest suitcase and, standing, swung it defiantly at the beast. *"No!"*

The ruse worked, and the scorpion shot out a pincher at Lauri. Dodging its grasp, she fell back to the ground. But as Lauri lifted her head, she heard more droning. The second scorpion came around the side of the Jeep and caught Lauri's motion.

Robert yelled, *"Lauri, RUN!"*

As the second scorpion headed straight for her, Lauri screamed and dashed away – the beast in pursuit.

The first scorpion came down on Robert and seized him with both pinchers. It twisted and yanked his body with massive force, tearing him away from his trapped leg. Robert yelled in agony and pushed against the nearest pincher with a final burst of strength – a move that riled the beast.

The last thing Robert ever saw was the scorpion's stinger whipping towards his chest.

Lauri had heard Robert's scream and, in tears, cried his name as she ran. With the second scorpion not far behind, she fled towards the end of the canyon. There, she saw several acres of primal clay that had eroded into a tall natural labyrinth. *The gorge!* Lauri glanced back to see the monster closing in then dashed for the maze. She shot into an open passage – the scorpion snapping its claws at her ankles.

In sheer terror, Lauri tore around a corner and rocketed down a narrower passage. The monster still followed but was slowed by having to partly crawl on the walls. As Lauri reached the path's end, the left wall was just low and wide enough for her to climb over. She rolled into the adjacent passage and gained a lead while the scorpion grappled with squeezing through.

Lauri ran around a bend and – now out of the monster's sight – sidestepped into a narrow cleft to hide. Holding her breath, Lauri watched as the monster shot past.

Quietly, the girl took deep breaths and waited as the beast's multiple footfalls faded away. In a few moments, her breathing returned to normal. Feeling a touch safer, Lauri cautiously stuck her head into the main passage to sneak a look.

No scorpion.

Lauri stepped partially out but hesitated, deciding whether to stay put or try to find a safer spot. *Leave well enough alone*, she reckoned and stepped back into the cleft.

But, at that instant, Lauri heard clicking, which echoed off the maze's walls. *Where's THAT coming from?*

She took a step outward, but the space around her grew darker. Lauri stopped and looked up. The scorpion was right above her, straddling the tops of the walls. It reached downward, and Lauri instantly fled. Now, the clefts were of no help. The beast had found a way to stalk her from above.

Seeing an opening, Lauri shot out of the maze and into a ravine – one encircled by walls of stone. She paused in the center, realizing it was a dead-end, then backed into a shadow – desperately looking for a way out.

The scorpion droned loudly as it crawled down from the top of the maze into the ravine. It searched about but saw nothing moving. Lauri froze, stifling her scream. She looked to her side and saw a jagged, climbable break running up the wall. Now, with the scorpion's back to her, Lauri made a beeline for the rift.

The scorpion heard her steps and turned. Just as Lauri started climbing, the beast saw her and shot forward.

Frantic, Lauri climbed as fast as she could. But as she neared the top, the scorpion stretched upward, extending its right pincher, and grabbed Lauri's ankle.

Lauri was dragged back down – wildly grasping at the wall's jagged edges.

The scorpion grabbed her ribs with its left pincher and turned her face up. The girl thrashed furiously. She yelled and used her free leg to repeatedly kick the pincher clamping her right foot.

The scorpion released Lauri's ankle then used the same pincher to grab her hips – firmly holding her horizontally. Peeved with Lauri's fighting, the monster chose to subdue its prey and began lifting its tail.

With the bright moonlight, Lauri could clearly see the stinger rising. Her eyes grew wide in fear, and she struggled even harder.

"No! ... *No!* ... *NO!*"

In a flash, the scorpion shot its tail forward – punching its stinger into Lauri's abdomen. As the air was knocked out of her, Lauri's head whipped back. The scorpion pushed down on its stinger – injecting more venom – and blood oozed up around the wound.

Lauri's abs began to jerk in spasms. She could feel the poison searing through her. Her muscles pulled taut. Her arms, wrists, and hands stiffened. Her knees bent, and her feet pointed in paralysis.

Finally, the monster withdrew its stinger, and Lauri was able to take in a long gasp of air. Her mind began spinning, and she lost her bearings. Now, all Lauri could lock on to was her rapidly pounding heart. Breathing in quick gasps, Lauri began to drip with sweat and shake uncontrollably. Her eyes darted wildly.

The scorpion slightly lifted Lauri's twitching body – raking its pincher towards her shoulders – then speared its stinger straight into her bare chest ... and bored down hard! Lauri's lungs filled, and a pint of luminous green venom erupted from her mouth. The poor girl's shaking ceased.

The beast pulled its stinger back and began to lift Lauri towards its oral cavity while extending its pair of slimy chelicerae – two long jaws, each ending in a pointed saw-toothed claw.

Slowly suffocating, Lauri could feel a thick burning liquid covering her lower torso and – after a moment – felt her abdomen being ripped open.

Her eyes rolled back. Her brain shorted out.

Like fireworks against a night sky, bursts of color splashed across Lauri's visual cortex ... then faded to darkness.

▶ At Desert Rocks, Al remained seated on his front porch – asleep.

In the picnic area, Dan, Tom, Yoli, and Billy were the only ones left – packing the last items into a few boxes. A very tired Dan said his goodnights and staggered to his Winnebago.

After entering, Dan paused by the door to massage his neck. He glanced over at Linda, who was already asleep in the front side-bed, and smiled. Removing his shirt, Dan walked towards the RV's back end.

He stopped at the open doorframe and looked in on the kids. Right away, Dan could see Patrick sleeping soundly. Then, he looked over at Jennie's bunk, where he saw what he took to be Jennie's sulking form slumbering beneath the covers. Dan sighed, regretting that he had needed to discipline her. He'd been yearning for Jennie to open up more to him, and *this* night certainly hadn't helped.

As Dan returned to the front, Patrick raised his head – looking up at the doorway and over at Jennie's bunk. He exhaled a sigh of relief.

Clad only in his BVDs, Dan crawled into bed with Linda. She instinctively turned, without waking, and snuggled close to him. Dan held Linda tightly, stroking her hair and kissing her forehead. He tried to fall asleep but couldn't. Dan stared into the darkness – wide awake.

▶ Not far from the fissure site, the two scouts were scurrying back to the nest – bearing scraps of prey for their young. The first scorpion carried Robert's right leg, while the second one bore Lauri's upper torso. They crawled over a hill and disappeared.

For the rest of the night, the desert was still.

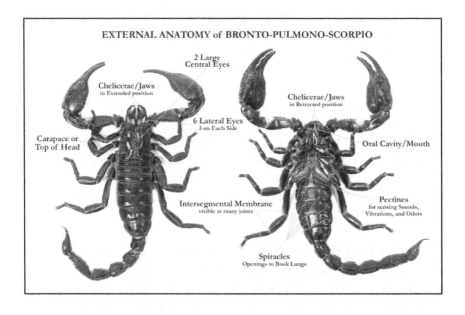

EXTERNAL ANATOMY of BRONTO-PULMONO-SCORPIO

2 Large
Central Eyes

Chelicerac/Jaws
in Extended position

Chelicerae/Jaws
in Retracted position

6 Lateral Eyes
3 on Each Side

Carapace or
Top of Head

Oral Cavity/Mouth

Intersegmental Membrane
visible at many joints

Pectines
for sensing Sounds,
Vibrations, and Odors

Spiracles
Openings to Book Lungs

48

PART TWO

Chapter 8

▶ As the sky gradually brightened before dawn, a light wind began to blow. Cautiously, Jennie returned to the campgrounds.

Inside their Winnebago, Dan and Linda still slept.

Patrick, however, was already dressed. He'd just finished making his bed when he turned and, looking through the window, saw Jennie approaching. Quickly, Patrick pulled the pillows out of her bed to make it look like she'd arisen earlier.

About 70 feet from the Winnie, Jennie paused and gulped. *Time to face the music.* She saw Patrick in the window, and he waved her forward. But, as Jennie neared the door, Patrick tapped the window and signaled for her to stop – silently mouthing the word "Wait!"

Gingerly, Patrick crutched up to the side door and glanced at his dozing parents. He very quietly opened the door and backed out of it, turning to Jennie and putting a finger to his lips.

Then Patrick leaned forward and cleared this throat as if he was coming in from the outside. "Morning, Dad."

Groggily, Dan struggled to open his eyes, "Hhuuuhh?"

"Jen 'n I rose early for a morning limp," explained Patrick, and he came in with Jennie following.

"Uuhh, that's nice." Smiling, Dan rolled over and fell back asleep.

The teens returned to the back room and plopped themselves on their respective beds. Jennie eyed Patrick suspiciously, but he just grinned and winked back at her. The girl cracked a slight smile, whispered "thank you," and collapsed onto her bunk.

▶ The sun rose over the eastern mountains and hit Al – still asleep on his porch – with its warm rays. Al gradually blinked awake. He felt the warm breeze then, alarmed, sat up straight.

Al stuck his head into Robert's room, calling for him. No one was there.

▶ A half-hour later, Dan found himself heading north on Highway 18, riding with Al and Tom in Al's Land-Ranger – a fully-equipped SUV that even sported sizeable sand-tires for firm off roading. As Al drove and Tom scanned the terrain, Dan sat in the back – next to a few Navajo blankets, a box of road flares, and a rack bearing a single shotgun.

The dry wind was now blowing a bit harder, and Dan took a swig from his canteen. "He could've just spent the night there."

Al shook his head. "It's not like him to make me wonder."

"But the land lines and mobiles are out," added Tom as they passed Box Canyon. "He couldn't 've called if he'd wanted." Tom looked forward and suddenly shouted, "Yikes!"

All three of them gasped at what they saw ahead – Dan shouting, "Al!'

Al slammed on his brakes.

"*Dios mio!*" cried Tom.

The Land-Ranger screeched to a halt just inches from a drop-off. Loose gravel on the very edge shot outward and tumbled into the ravine.

The bridge spanning Sand Canyon had collapsed, leaving a sheer drop to the wash below. On the other side, several long barricades with flashing yellow lights – obviously placed there by the Highridge police – barred access. But they were unmanned.

Dan, Tom, and Al took a collective breath. That was a close one. Carefully, Al backed up the Land-Ranger by several yards.

"Well, I guess we now know why Lauri's folks didn't make it last night," remarked Tom.

But a terrible possibility struck Dan, who shook his head. "Oh, no no! Just a second, here." He popped out of the Land-Ranger, followed by Tom and Al – the same thought hitting them.

The men carefully approached the edge of the cliff and peered down into the canyon.

Dan lowered himself to crawl on his belly to the very edge and look even further down. "Nothing but wrecked bridge."

"Thank heavens," sighed Al.

▶ The men returned on 18, driving the Land-Ranger slowly while intently scanning the countryside. As Al steered, Tom focused on one side while Dan scoped the other with his binoculars.

"You think the bridge could've collapsed *after* they crossed it?" asked Dan.

Al shook his head. "Most likely went down during the quakes."

Finally, Dan saw the Wrangler's tire tracks and pointed. "Hold it, Al! There 're tread marks headed off-road here."

Al stopped the Land-Ranger, stared intently, and nodded. "Those are Robert's tires, alright!" He drove into the terrain, following the tracks.

As they pushed forward, Dan also noticed what looked like hundreds of small footprints in the sand – on both sides of the Jeep's trail. *Were Robert and Lauri being chased? ... By what?!* Not wanting to alarm Al, Dan remained silent.

After they curved along Robert's trail, the overturned Jeep clearly came into view.

"Oh, no!" exclaimed Al. He stopped the Land-Ranger, jumped out, and ran forward.

Dan and Tom followed – Dan bringing his canteen and the shotgun.

Al saw what appeared to be Robert lying on the ground and ran towards him. "Oh my God, he's hurt! Robert!" But as Al grew closer, he slowed to a halt. On the ground lay Robert's remains. Seized by shock, Al could barely breathe.

There was a huge puncture in the center of Robert's chest. His eyes were frozen open. The flesh of Robert's lower torso had been eaten away – an exposed spinal cord trailing down to a bloody pelvis. And the disjointed bones of his arms were scattered about.

Al gasped for air and screamed, *"No!"* He fell to his knees and beat the earth. *"NO!"*

Dan and Tom caught up, both shaken to the core by what they saw. They looked at one another – each on the verge of tears.

Tom started to cross to Al. But Dan grabbed his arm, shaking his head and whispering, "He ... needs ... a few more minutes. There's nothing we can do, anyway."

"Where's Lauri?"

They looked about for the girl but only found Roberts's severed left leg, still pinned under the Jeep. Then, with the shotgun, Dan pointed out Lauri's footprints. "There. Looks like she ran that way. Stay here with Al." Dan walked off, following Lauri's tracks.

As Al alternated between wailing and catatonia, Tom knelt beside him. "Al."

The wind had not totally obliterated the footprints, and Dan tracked them towards the end of the canyon – also noticing the animal spoor alongside Lauri's prints. *What predator leaves tracks like these?*

He followed Lauri's trail into the labyrinth. There, Dan momentarily lost her footprints but, following his intuition, picked them up again. Finally, they led him into the dead-end ravine.

Dan's expression fell as he came upon Lauri's remains – a severed right leg, bare hip bone, and stripped left femur and tibia. Her broken left sandal and bloody ripped shorts lay nearby. The rest of her was missing.

Also, Dan noticed that Lauri's right leg displayed an unnatural pattern of cyanosis – a marbling of dark purple and cyan, with splotches of bright green. The very top of her thigh appeared black and mushy. Dan had noted that Robert's remains looked the same way, and it sickened him.

He turned, staggered, and braced himself against the rock wall – nearly passing out. Panting heavily, Dan opened his canteen and dowsed his head. After a moment, his breathing returned to normal.

Dan gathered his wits. He pushed his hair up from his eyes and started back for the crash site.

Minutes later, Dan approached Al and Tom, who were sitting next to the overturned Jeep. The wind had died to a mild breeze, and part of Al's sensibilities had returned.

Tom looked up as Dan arrived. "Lauri?"

Dan's ashen face said it all. "The same way."

With a gasp, Al buried his face in his hands.

Dan crossed to place a hand on his shoulder. "Oh God, Al, I'm ... I'm so sorry."

"I should have gone last night. Not the kids."

Tom quietly objected, "No, Al, don't–"

Al wept, and Dan and Tom remained quiet.

Then Dan tugged on Tom's sleeve, gently pulled him aside, and whispered, "Tom, what in God's name do you think did this? We *need* to know."

"Jeez, I've no idea," Tom softly responded. "Coyotes? Grizzlies? Javelinas, maybe?"

Al looked up and stared at them. "Mountain lions," he sobbed. "The climate change 's been wreaking havoc with them ... *Has* to be."

Tom stepped back towards Al. "More than one?!"

"To do this?" Al nodded, "Yes."

"That *could* explain the other tracks I've seen," added Dan. "But, if they're running in packs," Dan took in a gulp of air, "our *whole camp* could be in danger!"

Silently, Al and Tom stared at Dan – realizing he was right.

▶ Two hours later, Al rested on his living room sofa – a tearful Yoli wiping his forehead with a cool, wet cloth. Tom and a red-eyed Linda stood beside them.

"I, uh ... I'd better go help Dan." Tom turned to head through the kitchen to the back door.

Linda crossed to the dining room window and looked out at Al's Land-Ranger. Robert's Jeep – which Dan and Tom had up-righted and driven back – sat outside as well.

Linda saw Dan approaching Al's utility shed.

Dan opened the shed's door wide then moved to the Land-Ranger.

Tom stepped out of Al's back door to join him. "He's resting."

"Good," nodded Dan somberly.

Wrapped in the Navajo blankets, Robert and Lauri's remains lay in the back of the Land-Ranger. Tom hit an outer button that automatically opened the tailgate. Dan switched off the door light, reached in, and pulled Robert out.

Tom grabbed the blanket with Lauri's remains and dragged it away, spilling the box of road flares onto the cargo area.

He struggled to close the hatch, but Dan said, "Just leave it open. I killed the light."

Dan and Tom entered the shed and rested the bundles on the center table. As Dan checked Al's freezer for space, Tom grabbed a box of Hefty bags from a shelf.

54

Linda appeared at the door. "There's still no power."

"I know," replied Dan, "but this freezer should at least stay cool – somewhat." He moved back to the table.

Linda stepped inside. "Dan? ... I should look at them."

The two men froze, and Tom exclaimed, "Lady, this isn't something you want to see!"

"I didn't say I *wanted* to. I said I *should*."

Dan approached her. "God, Linda, why?!"

"To verify the bite patterns – teeth marks, whatever. I should be able to recognize *something*."

"You don't think it was mountain lions?" questioned Tom.

Linda grabbed a box of vinyl gloves off the shelf. "Just want to be certain that it *was*."

Dan approached her. "You sure, Linda?"

"I'll be fine. Give me ten minutes."

"Okay," agreed Dan.

As the men exited, Linda pulled on a pair of gloves and stepped towards the bundled remains.

Chapter 9

▶ "So, you think it was cougars?" asked Tom.

Robert's Jeep was parked under the shade of a desert palm. Dan and Linda sat in the back with Tom facing them from the front passenger seat. Dan grasped an open bottle of scotch. Linda held a shot glass.

"The rips *could* have come from claws, but there's–" Linda paused and lifted her glass towards Dan. "Hit me with another, will ya?"

Dan poured. Linda gulped.

She sighed and looked at the men, perplexed as hell. "The cyanosis of Robert's upper torso is unlike anything I've ever seen. There's extremely pronounced marbling ... and those *uncanny* streaks of bright green."

Dan nodded. "I saw that on Lauri, too."

"But what really baffles me," continued Linda, "is that some of Robert's flesh was partly liquefied."

"What?!" exclaimed Tom.

Dan asked, "And Lauri?"

Linda nodded. "Her leg shows the effects of venom, as well."

Tom questioned her logic. "Venom?"

"Rattlesnakes, maybe?" speculated Dan.

Linda shook her head.

"Aw, come on," argued Tom, "What else *could* it be but cougars?"

Linda flashed a defensive glare at Tom.

But Dan tried to make sense of it. "Linda, couldn't the green patches come from some kind of bacteria entering the wounds?"

Linda had enough of being doubted. "Oh now, *look*–"

"Hey, what's going on?" shouted an approaching Michael. "Everyone sees that somethin's up."

Tom turned to Michael, who now stood beside him. "Bro, we gotta grave situation here."

Dan and Tom rose and walked Michael away, with Dan explaining, "Yeah, and we need to *quietly* gather all the men into Al's living room."

Left alone, an irked Linda poured herself one last shot. "No *cat* did *this*."

► Al's bedroom doubled as his study. Besides his bed, the room was fitted with a desk, dresser, and large bookshelf. A samurai sword hung on one wall, along with tragic photos of Little Tokyo taken during *the relocation*. Al refused to forget what had happened back then. But, in contrast, his dresser-top was adorned with cheerful family photos.

Al had been sleeping for a while – lying on his bed, still clothed. Gradually, he grew aware of soft voices coming from his living room. As the words filtered into his consciousness, Al recognized Dan's voice.

"We believe the climate change has decimated the cats' food supply – forcing them downward, to stalk the high desert."

David added, "They're probably on edge from the quakes, too."

"Or maybe even rabid," suggested Gary.

"Well," said Tom, "whatever the reason, we can certainly assume that they're out there, banded together, and hungry!"

Though still grief-stricken, Al was now calm – past his initial surge of emotions. Slowly, he sat up on his bed and continued to listen.

"Then we gotta get out of here!" roared Frank.

"How?" questioned Michael. "18's blocked in both directions, 'n the rescue forces are all in San Berdoo!"

Al gathered his wits and pushed to his feet – the spinning in his head fading away.

► Dan, Tom, Jim, Mitch, David, Gary, Michael, Steve, and Frank were in the living room – all seated in a circle.

"The phone lines are all down," said Dan, "and no one has a signal on their mobile."

Frank asked, "Anyone have a C.B.?"

"Couple of us do," answered Tom. "Tried 'em, but no results. We're surrounded by mountains."

For a moment, the men paused in silence.

Then Steve Lacy asserted, "My Harley can make it over land."

"Not through Sand Canyon," contested Tom. "It's thick dry powder right now. You'll just dig in."

"And the surrounding terrain's all very rocky," came a weak voice from the hallway. Al approached the living room and paused in the doorway. "There's simply no practical way out of here."

"Al!" exclaimed Michael.

As the others reacted happily to Al's appearance, Steve shook his head in disagreement.

Jim stood and offered his chair. "Heavens, man, have a seat!"

Al nodded a thank you and sat down.

"You alright?" asked Dan.

"It's my duty to be part of this," affirmed Al, as Jim placed his hand on Al's shoulder.

But at that instant, Frank blurted, "Well, I sure don't wanna just sit around waiting to be next on the menu!"

The others gasped at Frank's disregard for Al's feelings.

"Jeez, bud!" Tom said, glaring at Frank.

But the shyster twaddled on, "Let's form a hunting party and track these bastards down ... right now!"

"It'll be dark soon," retorted Tom as he leaned forward, ready to punch him. "You wanna chase these cats at night?!"

Gently pulling down on Tom's shoulder, Dan intervened. "Let's post a *lookout* and take turns. We'll rotate each hour – sunset to sunrise."

"There's an observation deck on my roof," offered Al. "Gives a good view of the camp sites."

"Perfect," said Dan. "I'll go first. Then you, Frank – followed by Tom, Steve, Mitch, Gary, David, and Michael. That order okay?"

Everyone agreed, except Jim. "Well, what about me?"

Dan smiled. "How's your night vision?"

"Uh ... never mind."

Tom stood. "Al, we'll need to raid your armory."

As the others stood, Al raised his hands. "Well, hold it, everybody!" He began unlocking his rifle rack. "Tom, Dan – make sure any greenies here know what they're doing."

"Right, guys," agreed Tom, "we don't wanna go shooting each other."

"So if you *have* to fire," added Dan, crossing to the gun rack, "make sure that *no one* is *behind* your target!"

Dan took down one of the lever-action rifles and glanced at Al. "Marlin 357?"

Al nodded. "Holds ten shots."

"You got ammo?" asked Tom.

"Enough government issue for a small army," said Al, as he bent to unlock the cabinet below the rack, revealing a hundred boxes of rounds.

"Well, this *could* take down a cougar," said Dan as he handed the rifle to Tom, "and from a safe distance, too."

As Dan and Tom handed rifles and ammo to the rest, Al added, "Okay, but please ... everyone ... confine all activity just to the campgrounds!"

Yeah," affirmed Tom, "don't stray. We're definitely safer all together!"

As the men mumbled in agreement and started to exit, Dan made one last suggestion, "Oh, and uh, guys. Let's be *very tactful* in how we break all this to the women 'n kids."

▶ Tiffani was in screaming tears as she lay on the super coach's sofa – clutching her doll.

Margaret roared up from the kitchenette, raging into Frank's face. "Then you've got to get us out of here!"

"Oh, that'd be just fine," Frank yelled back. "You tell me how!"

Inside the Reyes' trailer, Michael and Elaine were somberly showering together by candlelight. As Michael tenderly shampooed his wife's long lovely hair, Elaine turned to face him.

Nearly in tears, the girl wiped the suds from her husband's shoulders. "Oh God, Michael." Elaine buried her head on his chest. "I just can't believe it."

They hugged each other tightly in solemn silence.

Chapter 10

▶ At dusk, Mitch, Kathy, David, and Gary were tossing around a football. Dan was on Al's roof, finishing the last minutes of his shift. Frank sauntered through the picnic area and approached Al's house, carrying his rifle. There to relieve Dan, he climbed Al's exterior ladder.

Dan was scanning the horizon with his binoculars when Frank's head popped up behind him.

"Anything?" asked Frank as he approached Dan.

Dan turned, glad to see him. "Just jackrabbits."

"Well, hand 'em over. I wanna get this done with."

Dan passed Frank the binoculars. "It's only for an hour."

Frank just grunted. Dan chuckled and descended the ladder.

▶ Outside the Winnebago, the Montgomery's generator was humming. Inside, Patrick, Billy, and Tiffani were seated around the dining table – enjoying multiple rounds of the latest hopped-up Pac-Man on Patrick's laptop. With her doll and a pile of dollars beside her, Tiffani had clearly mastered the joystick and was beating the pants off Patrick and Billy.

The boys weren't happy over being owned by a little girl.

"I thought you said you'd never played this before," moaned Billy – gently nudging her.

Tiffani rolled her eyes, "Stop whinin' 'n lay down your loot," then cracked a cute grin at him.

Awkwardly, Billy smiled back.

Yoli cracked-up over the little girl's sass.

But Margaret, seated beside her, was still stressed over the day's news – almost in tears. She reached over to touch Yoli's hand. "Thanks for asking Tiff over to play with the boys. She was a mess earlier. I still am."

"You might as well relax, Margaret. The guys 'll be watching out for us all night. Here." Yoli bent forward and refilled Margaret's glass from an icy pitcher. "Lemme top off that whisky slush."

Margaret broke a slight smile, nervously nodded, and sipped. "Ah, yes. I *do* need this."

▶ It was growing progressively darker, and Frank was becoming increasingly bored with scanning the terrain and witnessing nothing more than scampering hares. He sighed and tilted his binoculars into the campgrounds. *Surely, there's something more fun to watch down here.*

Frank followed Jim and Anne as they strolled about. Then, he swished the lenses over to the students as they tossed the football. He zeroed in on Kathy's tight cut-offs and slowly tilted down her legs. *Now THAT's more like it!*

▶ Linda and Dan sat with Al in his living room – Al silently staring into space. Linda looked over to Dan, and he nodded.

"Al," said Linda, breaking the silence, "I know it's hard to talk right now. But, I need to ask a few questions."

Al gazed at her, curious.

Linda continued, "You know I'm a veterinarian."

He nodded and looked down again.

"Well, could you remind me of which animals are common to this area ... especially the venomous ones?"

This puzzled Al. "Venomous?"

▶ Steve and Jennie quietly marched away from the campgrounds – pushing the Harley, with Steve's small backpack tied to the sissy bar.

"You leavin' your camp behind?" Jennie asked.

"Just the tent. Don't wanna tip anyone off."

They paused a good distance from the park – hidden by a large boulder – and mounted the bike.

Steve hit the ignition. He lifted Jennie's chin and gave her a tender kiss. "Once we get to safety, we'll bring back help."

Jennie smiled and nodded.

Slowly, they drove into the desert – running the engine as quietly as possible.

From Al's rooftop, Frank watched Steve and Jennie ride away. He lowered the binoculars. "Bright move, Brando!" Shaking his head, Frank glanced to the side. His eyes caught a warm light radiating from a back window in the Reyes' trailer, and he lifted the glasses. As Frank re-focused, his eyebrows shot up, and he whistled.

Through their bedroom window, Frank had a clear view of Michael and Elaine making love.

▶ Five candles wrapped the Reyes' bedroom in a soft orange glow – the setting completed by the soft instrumental Michael was playing on his boom box. He was on top of Elaine, and the two were passionately caressing and kissing.

Michael moved his mouth to Elaine's neck, where he flicked his tongue and nibbled on her ear lobe – carefully making sure to wrap his lips over his teeth to not hurt her. Elaine lightly moaned in response, and Michael gradually stepped down her neck in enduring kisses.

He ran his tongue across her shoulder – the scent of plumeria and the taste of coconut oil making her all the more delicious – and descended past her gold-cross necklace to her full, round breasts. Michael licked across Elaine's long cacao nipples and nibbled. Then, after gently pushing them together, he slowly ran his tongue along each areola, back and forth, in a figure-eight. The move delighted Elaine, and she giggled while massaging his shoulders.

Michael felt his member swelling and tapping against Elaine's moist gateway. *Not yet, buddy. We've more to do, first.* He moved his head lower and stepped down Elaine's tummy in a series of soft, lingering kisses.

Reaching Elaine's shaved mound, Michael was pleased, as always, by her small tattoo of a colorful butterfly. It was Elaine's sole body art – seen only by him – and Michael's temperature rose a degree each time he licked it. With one downward motion, his tongue was gently stroking her.

Elaine twisted and moaned, but Michael chose to tease her more.

He pulled his mouth away and ran his tongue slowly down her left leg to her toes. Gradually, he kissed his way back up to her knee. There, he licked up and down her thigh then began to gradually step kiss back upward.

But Elaine couldn't endure the teasing any longer. She moaned in angst, grabbed Michael's hair, and yanked his mouth back home.

Michael honed in on her swollen red bud – licking, sucking, gently nibbling – and, at the same time, placed his fingers on her nipples and lightly pinched.

Within moments, Elaine was crying out in an enduring orgasm.

Michael had chosen wisely when he set up camp a fair distance from the others. His sweet little bride was a *screamer* – and a loud one, at that.

Having her climax so vocally as his mouth pleasured her excited Michael a hundredfold. He continued until Elaine was begging him to stop – and then he went on for a bit more.

As she was catching her breath, Michael paused and rose – preparing for entry. Elaine lifted her hips to receive him and gasped upon penetration. As they held each other tightly, Michael began moving in a long slow rhythm and then picked up speed.

Looking through his binoculars, leaning left and right to follow the action, Frank took in every detail.

Elaine arched back. Her head fell off the bed and her body quivered with each of Michael's thrusts.

"Hmmm-mmm," said Frank to himself, cracking a lecherous grin and lighting a cigarette.

▶ Dan had moved to Al's front porch for some fresh air.

Inside, Al was answering Linda's question. "Rattlers won't attack unless you surprise them. Same for the tarantulas, but their bite's harmless. And the black widows I pretty well eradicate."

"Any others?"

"Scorpions."

Linda's eyes lit up.

Al continued, "Those six-inchers aren't very poisonous. It's the tiny yellow ones that 'r bad news. But you don't find many here in ..." he paused, his mind returning to his grief, "... in the high desert." Al sighed and leaned back to rest.

Linda paused in thought.

▶ Yoli opened the door of the Winnebago. Margaret and Tiffani stepped out – the child clutching her doll and her winnings. Now, as Tiffani counted the dollars, Margaret was clearly more relaxed.

"Well bye, Yoli," said Margaret. "And thanks."

The giggling voices of Billy and Patrick could be heard teasing from inside. "Take her away! She's cleaned us out!"

Laughing as she closed the door, Yoli looked back at them and said, "Well boys, don't ever underestimate a pretty little girl."

Margaret clucked and looked down at her daughter.

Proud of herself, Tiffani looked up at her mom but noticed the newly-risen full moon. "Ah, mommy, look! The moon's so big and ... *orange!*"

"Yes, honey. It looks bigger when it's rising." Margaret took a deep breath, relaxing even more. "The sky's so clear here. Wanna take the back trail to our camp?"

"Oh-kay!"

As they strolled into the pathway, Tiffani resumed counting her dough. "Ya know, I could make a livin' doin' this."

Margaret laughed. "Well, stop braggin' and watch your step, sweetie. This trail's full of rocks."

▶ Binoculars raised and with a cigarette now dangling from his lips, Frank continued spying on the Reyeses – the show being way too good to turn away from. Through the window, Frank saw the lovers switch positions – with Elaine now riding Michael like a bucking bull.

The girl moaned.

Head resting on the pillow, Michael was consumed by the sight of his bride – her heart-shaped face, deep brown eyes, flowing hair, her bosom dancing above her waist, and her hips encircling him. He licked his fingers and began massaging Elaine below her butterfly.

She came again. And Michael, who'd held back until now, exploded. Each emitted a loud, enduring cry.

Elaine collapsed on top of him, draping her leg over the edge of their bed – cinnamon skin against white sheets.

And through his specs, Frank could see them hugging each other tightly.

As Elaine fell asleep in his arms, Michael smiled – wholly contented and at peace. He closed his eyes and kissed Elaine on the forehead, imagining how beautiful the child they'd worked to conceive would be.

Remembering that he needed to snuff the candles, Michael slowly opened his eyes. They focused on their open window and, at that moment, Michael caught the glowing tip of Frank's cigarette in the distance. The light of the full moon told him the rest – especially its glint off the binoculars' glass.

Pure outrage flashed through Michael – but only for a second. It was impossible for him to be angry while holding Elaine.

After taking a deep breath, Michael now felt more pity for Frank than anything else. But sympathy morphed into amusement, and a big toothy grin spread across Michael's face. Slowly, he began to lift his free arm.

Through the binoculars, Frank saw Michael lift his arm and make a fist. And in the next instant, Michael thrust his fist forward and extended his middle finger.

Shocked at being discovered, Frank abruptly swiveled away and lowered the glasses.

Michael quietly chuckled. Without waking Elaine, he gently rose, snuffed the candles, and returned to her side.

Not only was Frank worried over what Michael might do, he felt ashamed ... and empty. He had longed to experience the kind of innocent passion the Reyeses enjoyed, but such feelings had fled his marriage long ago. Now, Frank's ego was warping his shame into anger and jealousy.

Suddenly, though, Frank paused – distracted. He realized that something was different. *What the–? Wait!* He looked around the grounds, and then it hit him. The typical sounds of the desert night – particularly the chirping of the crickets – had completely halted. Other than the noise made by the football-tossing students, it was dead quiet. *Now THAT is weird!*

▶ Al sat alone in his living room, head buried in his hands.

Linda was speaking with Dan on the front porch. "It was at the zoo. We had a small desert scorpion – a Centruroides. Kevin was careless in cleaning the display and got stung. His wound didn't swell, but the skin around it turned that same bright green. And he got very sick."

"Okay," nodded Dan, "but for Robert and Lauri to have looked the way they did, they'd have to have been stung by an entire nest."

Linda stopped cold. She raised a hand to her head and exhaled a distressed laugh. "Now that's really odd."

"What?"

Deep in thought, Linda turned and stepped to the porch's edge – facing the soft moonlight. "That big round wound in Robert's chest. It wasn't swollen either."

As she glanced up and outward, Linda froze. The reflection of the full moon in her eyes was blotted out. She gasped at what she saw and tried to speak but, fighting to catch her breath, could not. Finally, Linda emitted a bloodcurdling scream!

Silhouetted against the moon, the huge black Bull Scorpion was poised on top of the nearby hill.

Chapter 11

▶ On Al's roof, Frank heard Linda's scream and looked up. He beheld the Bull Scorpion too and, like Linda, froze – convinced his eyes were fooling him.

The creature had paused on the hilltop and, with his hind legs stretched, was surveying the terrain below. He saw movement.

As other scorpions began to appear from behind him, the Bull extended his right pincher and stepped back – droning his scouts forward. One by one, they began to descend into the campgrounds.

Frank shook himself into action. He grabbed his Marlin to fire a warning, but it only clicked. "What the–?!" Realizing he hadn't loaded the rifle, Frank grabbed a box of ammo and started fumbling.

Al stepped onto his porch and sighted the creatures – freezing, like the others, in disbelief.

Dan shouted up to the roof. "FRANK!"

While loading his rifle, Frank yelled at the top of his lungs, "Everyone, take cover! Scorpions!"

▶ The four students stopped throwing their football and turned around to see Frank yelling, "HUGE scorpions! Everybody inside!"

Mitch took it as a joke. "*What* did he say?"

The youths bunched together and lifted Kathy's phone to take a selfie of them laughing with Frank screaming from the roof above.

All of a sudden, there was a loud droning, followed by a roaring hiss. The students looked up, and a scorpion came around two large boulders. The beast turned and spied the kids. Another scorpion crept up to join the first and was followed by two more. The bright moonlight fully revealed the creatures' repulsive features. Kathy screamed, and the scorpions scuttled towards her.

The students fled – Gary crying, "Jesus Christ!"

Gary and David peeled-off in one direction and Mitch and Kathy in another.

▶ Snapping to his senses, Al yelled at everyone. "Take cover! Grab your weapons!" He ran inside to fetch his rifle.

Dan checked his Marlin, looked at Linda, and nodded at Al's door. "Stay in there. I'll check on the kids."

Al joined Dan, and they ran towards the picnic area.

But Linda was fearful. "Dan?!"

He paused to yell back at her, and he meant business. *"GET INSIDE AND CLOSE THE DAMNED DOORS!"*

And she damned-well did.

▶ Mitch and Kathy ran across the campgrounds. Behind them, two scorpions dashed in pursuit – one well ahead of the other.

While Kathy moved on, Mitch paused to throw his football at the head of the nearest monster. It bounced off, momentarily halting the beast's charge.

Kathy stopped to look back. "Mitch!"

"Get my pistol!" Mitch yelled. He hurled a stone at the monster and ran on.

But as Mitch raced to catch up with Kathy, the leading scorpion closed in and grabbed him. Struggling futilely, Mitch cried out as the beast lifted him.

Kathy paused again and looked back to see the monster driving its stinger into Mitch's body. "NO!"

And in that instant, the second scorpion caught up and bolted straight towards her.

Helpless, Kathy had no choice but to flee.

▶ On the back trail, Margaret and Tiffani were returning to their camp when they heard the commotion.

They froze in their tracks as they saw a giant scorpion approaching. Tiffani screamed, and the scorpion lurched forward. Margaret snapped to her senses, grabbed her daughter's hand, and ran off.

Jim and Anne Johnson strolled around a corner – with Anne glancing at Jim and asking, "Can you make out what everyone's shouting?"

Upon hearing and downright *feeling* a droning, the Johnsons halted. Margaret and Tiffani ran directly past them. Tiffani tripped. Margaret picked her up and fled – the scorpion close behind.

Jim gasped, "Whoa dog–!" Anne had clamped his mouth shut.

As another scorpion scouted through the terrain, Jim and Anne slowly and quietly backed up and hid in back of a huge boulder.

Anne whispered, "Don't ... move ... or make ... a sound."

▶ In the central campground, a single scorpion was tearing into Steve's empty tent. Dan and Al bolted forward then hunkered down at a distance. While a second scorpion appeared from behind Steve's camp, the first one saw the two men and charged. Dan and Al began firing their rifles.

▶ Inside their trailer, Michael and Elaine – who had been cuddled together, sleeping – were awakened by the sound of close gunfire.

"Michael?!"

The young man stood and crossed to the window. But since they had isolated themselves around a bend from the main group, large boulders blocked his view. "Can't see anything from here ... 'cept for that wanker on Al's rooftop!"

▶ Because their Mustang's top was down, Kathy made a bee-line for her tent. Once inside, she zipped up the opening. The pursuing scorpion scuttled right up to the tent and paused, puzzled by the cocoon its prey had vanished into.

Carelessly, Kathy switched on an LED lantern to aid her search through Mitch's bag – not realizing the lamp projected her shadow onto the very canvas the monster was facing. Once the beast saw movement, it lunged at the fabric.

Kathy found Mitch's revolver and whipped around, taking aim. She fired all five rounds, but the beast gave them no heed and tore through the canvas. Panicking, Kathy threw the pistol straight at its head and tried to scramble out from under the tent wall. With the gun smashing one of its eyes, the beast flew it into a rage and reached forward.

Kathy's head popped out from under the canvas but, as the girl tried to scrabble through, the scorpion caught her leg and yanked her back inside.

69

Screaming, Kathy tried to twist free. The monster seized her shoulder and fired its stinger straight into her neck, killing her scream in a gurgle. Then it forcefully jerked back its tail, tearing off Kathy's head.

▶ Combining their rifle fire, Dan and Al had been able to keep the scorpion that destroyed Steve's tent from advancing on them. But the second scorpion now crawled forward to join him.

Unexpectedly, Dan's rifle jammed, and both of the scorpions began to close in.

Hoping to buy Dan some time, Tom stepped out from his van and began firing *his* rifle at the beasts.

With Tom entering the fray, the creatures halted a moment then split up. The first scorpion rushed towards Dan while the second went for Tom.

Al backed off to the side but couldn't shoot. "You're in my line of fire! Run!"

Dan bolted for Al's house with the scorpion four lengths behind him. Tom dashed to the Winnebago – the second beast right on his tail.

While fleeing, Dan glanced back to see what was happening.

Yoli swung open the Winnie's door, letting in Tom, and slammed it just in time. The monster halted, scraping its pincher on the door. It backed off a few yards and stared at the RV in confusion.

Dan was nearing Al's house.

On Al's rooftop, Frank had just finished loading his Marlin. He saw Dan coming, took aim at the monster, and fired. Distracted by the bullet, the scorpion turned about to see what had stung him.

Dan reached the porch and paused again to look back, shouting, "Al!"

But from where he stood, Al could hear cries for help from David, Gary, and Margaret. He pivoted and headed deeper into the campgrounds.

At a window in the Winnebago, Tom and Patrick breathed a sigh of relief as they saw Linda swing open Al's front door and yank Dan inside.

As soon as Linda slammed the door, she had her arms around him.

70

▶ Al ran forward and arrived at the student's campsites. He saw the scorpion devouring Kathy just outside her partly collapsed tent. It had severed the girl and was munching on her headless upper torso. Kathy's legs and lower torso lay on the ground beneath.

As Al backed off in revulsion, he heard two voices crying out. "Help!" "Help us!" Al turned to see David and Gary running his way with a scorpion in pursuit.

He fired his rifle at the creature, momentarily distracting it, then shouted, "Get in your van 'n don't move!"

While the boys entered the safety of the van, Al fired at the beast again. He yelled to grab its attention and then dashed away – the scorpion now following *him*.

▶ Margaret came stumbling headlong around a curve, carrying Tiffani, when her foot caught one of the path's stones, and she slammed into the ground. Tiffani tumbled away – her dollar bills flying all about.

Margaret heard the pursuing scorpion drawing near and looked up.

The beast hadn't seen them fall – so, on catching up, it momentarily paused to take in what had happened.

Tiffani began to cry, and the scorpion turned towards her.

Swiftly, Margaret jumped up and began waving her arms – yelling to distract the beast. "Tiffani! Don't move! If it comes at me, get in the coach!"

Her gambit worked. The scorpion lunged at Margaret, and she fled with the beast in pursuit.

Clutching her doll, Tiffani stood and yelped. Her right leg had been hurt. Tiffani limped over to the super coach, but it was locked. She pounded on the door, crying, "Daddy! Open the door!"

Suddenly, Tiffani heard another loud droning. She turned to see the Bull Scorpion stalking by. The terrified girl caught her scream then slowly crawled underneath the super coach and hid beside a tire. As she silently cried and hugged her doll, Tiffani watched the brute saunter away.

▶ Inside the Reyes trailer, Michael and Elaine heard the droning and hissing but had not caught sight of the beasts.

"I've never heard big cats sound like *that!*" said Michael while pulling on his trousers.

Frightened by the unearthly sounds, Elaine drew the sheets protectively up around her.

"Hey, it's okay." Michael moved back to hold her tightly and whispered. "We'll just stay quiet."

Chapter 12

▶ Yelling, Margaret fled towards Al's house. "Frank!"

From the rooftop, Frank saw her coming – a scorpion in pursuit! "Jesus, Margaret!"

As his wife drew closer, Frank fired at the monster. The bullet momentarily stung it, buying Margaret more distance. Frank fired once more, then ran to the ladder and scrambled down.

He met Margaret on Al's front porch and, as Dan opened the door, dragged her inside. The scorpion scurried up onto the porch and ransacked it, finding nothing. Frustrated, it crept away.

From Al's dark living room window, Dan, Linda, Frank, and Margaret watched the monster depart.

Panting deeply, Margaret grabbed Frank. "Frank! Tiffani's out there!"

"What?!"

"I led it away, but I ... I realize she can't get in! The coach's locked!" Margaret began crying. "Get my baby, Frank!" She pressed her hands on the window, looking outward in hysterics. "Go get my baby!"

Frank paused next to her, stunned.

▶ Tiffani remained hidden under the super coach, whimpering by the tire. The Bull Scorpion returned, passing through the area again – droning. It paused, sensing nearby prey.

Terrified, Tiffani shoved her fist into her mouth – stifling her scream.

The Bull couldn't tune in to where the tasty little morsel was hidden. But he heard the nearby droning of one of his scouts, droned back in response, and moved on.

▶ Having ditched the scorpion that was chasing him, Al had stumbled upon Jim and Anne Johnson. Now, he was escorting them back to their trailer – cautiously scrambling from one boulder to another.

They were paused behind a big rock that was about 120 feet from the door of the Johnson's small Silverstream. As Al peered past the boulder, he saw a scout prowling the grounds on the other side – right between them and the trailer.

Al whispered to Jim and Anne, "Once that bastard's past, I'll run ahead to cover you. When I signal, follow me 'n get in your trailer – quick!"

Jim and Anne nodded.

The creature moved away and rounded a corner. Al waited a moment to make sure it was gone then quietly crept out. He paused mid-way to look around. The coast was clear, so he waved the Johnsons on.

As they hustled past Al, Jim whispered, "How we doin'?

"Fine. Just head on inside."

The Johnsons rushed to their trailer as Al guarded the rear. But just as Jim and Anne neared their door, two scorpions scurried into the open, turned, and caught sight of them.

Al yelled at Jim and Anne, "Get in there," then stepped towards the scorpions, raising his rifle.

The creatures started for him.

Jim entered the trailer, but Anne paused at the door. "Al!"

Though Al fired at the scorpions, they kept coming. He glanced at Anne. "GET INSIDE!"

As Anne stepped in, the scorpions charged. Al fired once more, but the beasts moved so rapidly that they cut Al off from the door. He had no choice but to turn and flee.

▶ Margaret anxiously peered out of Al's living room window as Dan and Frank reloaded their rifles.

"For Christ's sake," said Linda, crossing to Dan, "don't go out there again!"

"Shut up, damn you!" snapped Margaret. "My child's in danger!"

Outside, Al scrambled towards his house – the two scorpions rapidly closing in on him.

"Help me!"

In the living room, the people heard Al drawing closer.

"Dan!"

They crossed to the window to see Al nearing the front porch.

"Open up!"

Frank and Dan shot to the door.

Dan stepped out onto the porch and fired a few rounds at the beasts. Al dashed inside, and Dan and Frank followed him – with Frank slamming the door and Dan locking it.

Thwarted, the scorpions scrounged about the porch then stepped back and paused – facing the house and waiting. Whatever this *hive structure* was, they now realized their prey was inside of it.

In the connected dining room, Dan and Frank propped up a very winded Al. Linda crossed to give him a hug.

"Our bullets hardly faze them!" panted Al.

Margaret had remained at the living room window, looking out at the beasts. Seeing that the scorpions were remaining just outside the house, she grew hysterical. "No. No, go away!"

The others joined her at the window.

Outside, two more scorpions – one of them being the droning Bull – joined the first two. They encircled Al's house, one facing each wall, and remained still – waiting.

▶ Two scorpions had rustled up onto the roof of the Montgomery's Winnebago. Though the sound of their outside generator had initially attracted them, its fuel gauge was now reading empty. Burning its last fumes, the generator sputtered and started to die.

Inside the RV, Patrick, Tom, Yoli, and Billy were huddled around Patrick's computer – which beeped as it switched to battery. The single dim nightlight they'd been burning now faded. And, as Patrick closed his laptop, they heard the scorpions scuttling about the roof.

Tom whispered, "Don't anyone move. Not a sound."

There was a moment of quiet. Then, unexpectedly, one of the scorpions made a loud, fast scrabble to the front of the RV. The people saw the beast's grotesque underside shoot down, past the windshield, to the ground. Billy gasped, but Tom clamped his mouth.

Both scorpions paused – one on the roof and one on the ground – patiently waiting for a noise or movement to come from the Winnie.

And inside, everyone gaped at one another in dead silence.

▶ Four miles West, a frustrated Steve Lacy was piloting his Harley through rough sandy terrain – Jennie hugging on to his back. He'd not gotten as far as hoped, but he was not about to give up either.

Occasionally, they had broken into clear stretches and made up some time. They had just hit one of those tracts and were moving briskly along when, suddenly, they reacted in horror to what lay ahead.

Terrified, Jennie cried, "Steve?!?"

Steve braked the Harley to a dead stop – a mere 30 feet before a 12-foot scorpion. Another one was approaching from their side.

"Holy shit!" Steve looked around then fired the Harley in the only direction he had open – shooting towards a large outcropping of inclined rocks.

As they fled, the Harley swerved in the powder – however, Steve regained control. He looked back to see the gaining scorpions and gunned the bike to gain speed. But with Jennie's weight on his back, the rear wheel pushed them up into an unwanted wheelie. They fell off the Harley, and the bike somersaulted into a boulder.

Recovering, Steve and Jennie saw the two scorpions drawing closer. They dashed to the slanted rocks.

"We gotta scale this incline!" Steve took Jennie by the arm and pulled her up onto a bed of basalt. "Their own weight'll keep 'em down."

On the second level of basalt, they reached the base of the slant. Tiring, Jennie slowed, so Steve started pushing her up ahead of him. A loud hiss made Steve glance back. The nearest scorpion was almost on top of them.

To save Jennie, Steve gave her a huge shove. "Get up there, FAST!"

Jennie scrambled upwards. And as Steve started to follow, he was seized by the first scorpion. The beast yanked the boy back and wasted no time in stinging him. As the poison burned through Steve, he yelled in pain and began shaking. Jennie screamed at the sight, but the second scorpion was barreling straight for her.

76

Frantic, Jennie continued upward – nearing the peak. The incline grew steeper and, while the scorpion was able to continue forward, it *did* have to slow down.

Likewise, the steepness caused Jennie to lose her footing. The girl slipped and began sliding downward. She twisted and looked down to see herself hurtling towards the monster. The scorpion raised its pinchers – ready to catch her. Jennie wailed and covered her eyes.

But the momentum of Jennie's fall was so great that the beast couldn't grab her fast enough. She slid through, beneath the monster – scraping its pectines – and continued downward.

Jennie opened her eyes to find herself shooting straight towards a gap between the incline and a wall of basalt. She smashed into the rock, lost consciousness, and fell through the gap – down eight feet – onto the dirt floor of a stone alcove.

The scorpion scuttled down to the opening and stretched its hind legs to look inside. It tried to reach in, but the opening was too narrow for its pinchers. Thwarted, the monster turned about – clenching its pinchers in anger – then looked back down into the crevasse in frustration.

Chapter 13

▶ Outside Al's home, two of the four scorpions left in search of easier prey. One scout remained in the yard to watch the house, and the Bull Scorpion climbed up onto Al's roof. He rummaged about the observation deck then crept over to the roof's other side.

▶ Michael and Elaine remained in their trailer's bedroom, listening to the commotion but seeing nothing. Then, abruptly, they heard something shuffling above them, and their heads snapped upwards.

Outside, a scorpion had paused on their trailer's roof. A second, slightly larger, scout crawled up from a boulder behind the trailer and joined the first. The monsters droned at each other, agreeing that these *hives* contained prey.

Not knowing what truly waited outside, Michael stood, banged on the ceiling, and yelled. Bad move. The noise and vibrations gave them away.

The scorpions dropped to the ground and, each grabbing an opposite end, began to tilt the *hive*.

Fortunately, the boulder blocked the trailer from fully tipping over. But inside, Michael and Elaine fell against the wall.

Michael flew into a rage. "Cougars, Hell! Someone's fuckin' with us!" He grabbed his rifle. "And I know just *who!*"

Elaine balanced herself and donned a short silk robe as Michael, straddling the wall and floor, stumbled down the center of the skewed trailer.

He kicked the door open and jumped outside to the ground. "All right, you bastards!" As Michael swung around, he froze, trying to make sense of what he saw.

The two huge scorpions had been searching for prey beneath the vehicle. But now, on seeing Michael, they moved out from under it – allowing the trailer to upright itself.

"*Aking Dios!*" Michael backed up as the scorpions slowly approached him.

Elaine appeared at the doorway, saw the two monsters nearing her husband, and gasped – unable to even scream.

Taking control, Michael raised his rifle and shouted, "Lock yourself inside, Elaine!" He stepped sideways to avoid hitting her then fired several times. But the scorpions were unfazed. They seized Michael so swiftly, he was barely able to scream.

Seeing her husband stung, Elaine found her voice and shrieked, "*Ginoo ko!*" She ran back inside and yanked open a small closet.

As the venom sent Michael into convulsions, the two scorpions began fighting over him – the smaller one grabbing at him while the larger beast yanked him away. And now, attracted by the clamor, two more scorpions entered the fray.

Elaine pulled a ball bat from the closet and dashed back to the door.

Screaming, "Michael," she dashed outside with the bat raised – but the two new monsters pounced on her. The brave girl swung repeatedly, smacking their claws.

Alas, there was no way to save Michael now.

Just then, one of the scorpions seized the bat and yanked it from Elaine's hands. She dodged the other beast's pinchers and retreated into the trailer. The beast with the bat dropped it and grabbed the door.

Elaine flew down the length of the trailer. She paused at the bedroom entrance and looked back to see two pinchers tearing the door from its hinges.

Now, in a frenzy, the two scorpions began ripping the door frame apart. Having caught Elaine's scent, they were not about to let such luscious prey escape them.

With a scream, Elaine threw herself into the bedroom. She slid the door shut and piled their suitcases and mattress in front of it. In pure panic, Elaine huddled in a corner and began to cry.

Outside, the first two scorpions continued fighting over Michael's limp body. The larger scorpion succeeded in forcing the smaller one back. He ripped Michaels' right arm clean off, tossed it aside, and shoved his bleeding socket up to its oral cavity. The smaller scorpion snuck back and snatched the discarded limb for itself.

▶ Beneath the Stewart's super coach, Tiffani was now quiet – and so were the immediate surroundings. The little girl leaned forward and looked out past the tire she was hiding behind. No scorpions.

Tiffani pulled back and whimpered, wondering why Margaret had not returned for her.

▶ The four scorpions were still outside of the Reyes' trailer. While the first pair ravenously tore Michael apart, the second two finished shredding the vehicle's door frame. Now, with the opening wide enough, they scrambled into the trailer.

Inside, the monsters quickly traced Elaine's scent towards the back.

From the bedroom corner, Elaine could hear them scuffling forward. She held her breath.

BANG! The sliding door was hit hard! Elaine jumped – her eyes wide as saucers. A pincher started to break through.

Elaine looked up at a window then over at her night case. Without missing a beat, the girl rose, grabbed the case, and used it to pound out the window. In three whacks, the metal frame fell outside. And just as the scorpions smashed through the doorway, Elaine pulled herself up and slid through the opening.

Landing barefoot on the ground, she glanced about, desperate to find safety, as the scorpions inside the trailer droned in annoyance. Elaine crossed the back of the trailer, warily peeked around the corner, and saw the first two beasts feasting on Michael. She turned away, tears streaming down her cheeks.

But Elaine knew she had no time to waste. Driven by instinct, her goal was now to save herself and the child growing within her. She fled towards the central campgrounds.

A cacophony of droning shook the air. Hearing a scorpion drawing near, Elaine scooted ahead and hid in the shadow of a large boulder – peeking over the top to watch it pass. After she saw the monster join the others at her trailer, she moved on.

Cautiously, Elaine approached the ranger booth near Al's house. She paused inside and, tears still flowing, leaned against the wall to collect her wits. A moment later, she heard another droning and looked around the side of the booth.

The scout remaining in Al's yard had finally grown impatient and headed off to seek new prey.

And from the darkness of Al's kitchen window, Dan also watched the scorpion depart.

▶ Still waiting for her mother, Tiffani feared that a scorpion would soon find her.

She peeked around the tire again and, with no monster in sight, began to whimper. "Mommy?!" Impatient, Tiffani crawled out from underneath the super coach. With her leg still hurting, she limped into the open and glanced about. "Mommy?!"

▶ Elaine had watched the scout leave Al's yard. Certain that he was gone, the girl stepped out of the guard booth – planning to head for the safety of Al's house.

From Al's kitchen window, Dan was also convinced the scorpion had left. At that moment, he spotted Elaine hesitating by the booth.

Dan hefted his rifle and opened Al's back door. He waved at the girl to come over. "Elaine!"

Elaine looked at Dan, took a timid step forward, then glanced about fearfully. The coast seemed clear, so she continued on. But halfway, Elaine heard a crying child. She paused, looked to her side, and spied Tiffani.

"Mommy?!" The little girl was limping aimlessly through the picnic area, clutching her doll and weeping. "Mommy?!"

Peering into the shadows beyond, Elaine saw a large black form growing closer – a scorpion heading straight for the child!

"Tiffani!" Elaine dashed off.

Seeing that she'd diverted, Dan stepped outside.

As the scout closed in, Elaine scooped up the little girl and then sprinted for the house.

Dan cocked his Marlin and yelled, "Faster! I'll cover you!"

He moved away from the house to clear his line of fire – passing the open tailgate of Al's Land-Ranger and seeing the spilled road flares in back. After firing two ineffective rounds, Dan grabbed a flare, yanked off its seal, and looked back up.

Carrying Tiffani, Elaine ran towards Dan and Al's back door – the scout giving chase.

Linda, Al, Margaret, and Frank watched through the side dining room window.

Margaret squealed, "It's Tiffani!"

Frank's eyes lit up, and he and Al moved to the kitchen – with Frank pausing at the kitchen window and Al standing by the door.

Dan ignited the flare, dashed towards Elaine, then paused at the edge of the yard. As Elaine dashed past, Dan shoved the flare up in front of him.

To the scout's eyes, the burning flare grew into a blinding supernova.

The beast halted and stepped back, with Dan successfully holding it at bay.

Elaine drew closer to Al's back door.

▶ As Al started to open the door, Frank rushed him. "Outta my way!"

Al grabbed his shoulder. "Wait, let her in first!"

But Frank shoved Al to the floor and ran outside.

He met Elaine several yards out and yanked Tiffani from her arms, "Give 'er to me!"

"Daddy!"

Elaine was crushed as Frank, without even a nod of thanks, turned his back on her.

Suddenly, a loud *hiss* came from above, and Elaine looked up.

The Bull Scorpion shot down from the roof, straight at her.

Clutching Tiffani, Frank flew back inside and slammed the door.

Elaine fell backwards and just missed being grabbed. She scrambled to her feet and dashed around the back of the house. The Bull lost a few seconds in getting all of his legs to the ground but then shot off in pursuit.

Dan had now held the scout for as long as he could. The flare was beginning to die, and the scout's eyes were adjusting. With the beast starting to inch forward, Dan threw the flare at its eyes and ran for the back door. He flew into Al's kitchen.

Al slammed the door, and Linda crossed to hug Dan.

Margaret grabbed Tiffani from Frank. "My baby!"

But Dan looked about, alarmed. "Where's Elaine?"

"Yeah!" Fuming, Al grabbed Frank and slammed him against the wall. "Where *is* Elaine?!"

Chapter 14

▶ In sheer terror, Elaine had dashed around the other side of Al's house and fled – screaming – towards the central campgrounds. She'd gained a good lead over the Bull Scorpion, though it was still in dogged pursuit.

Inside their Silverstream, Jim and Anne Johnson heard the girl's screams drawing closer. They looked out their window in horror.

Not far from their trailer, Elaine paused to catch her breath. She glanced back at the swiftly approaching Bull.

Jim and Anne opened their door – both calling, "Elaine! Over here!"

Elaine made a mad dash for their door. But as she got closer, a scout scuttled out from behind the trailer – cutting her off. She screamed to a halt, looked back at the Bull, then dashed towards a trailhead.

Seeing Elaine divert, Jim stepped out. "Elaine!?"

But Anne saw the scout making for Jim and yanked him back inside, slamming the door not a moment too soon.

The Bull charged through in pursuit of Elaine. And the scout remained at the Silverstream, wondering how to crack the big egg its prey had drawn into.

▶ With more scouts now sniffing about Al's house and every vehicle, Elaine had no choice but to flee the campgrounds. She dashed down the trail that led to Hidden Valley, hoping to find cover in its many boulders. But Elaine knew that she first had to get out of the beast's direct view. To do so called for her to widen her lead. She ran furiously.

▶ Spotlit by moonlight beaming through their trailer window, Jim and Anne were hugging.

Anne softly wept and looked up at Jim. "What can we do?"

Jim silently shook his head and hugged her tightly.

The moonlight was suddenly cut off as the hissing scout, searching for a way in, crawled up past the window to their roof. The Johnsons held their breaths and pulled back into the shadows.

▶ Her heart pounding, Elaine shot down the rocky hiking trail with the Bull Scorpion hot on her heels. She could hear the beast gaining, so she aimed for the nearest rocks.

But the Bull was wholly focused on seizing the prey it desperately needed. Closing in, he could nearly taste the girl. The monster accelerated and extended his arms.

As Elaine darted between two boulders, the Bull thrust its right pincher forward and caught her. Screaming at the top of her lungs, she was lifted back.

Elaine struggled furiously in the beast's pincher and managed to deftly twist her small frame just enough to slip from its grasp. The bottom of her robe caught on the jagged edge of the claw but luckily tore, and Elaine fell.

She hit the ground and found herself gaping straight up into the monster's oral cavity – her face merely two-and-a-half feet from its slimy serrated jaws.

Aghast, Elaine turned and began to scramble away. But the Bull swiftly pinned her neck and shoulders to the ground.

With her legs clambering freely, Elaine again tried to force her way out of the beast's grip. So the Bull then clamped her thighs with its free pincher. Now, no matter how hard she fought, Elaine wasn't going anywhere.

The Bull raised his tail – the tip of its stinger dripping venom – and yanked up Elaine's shoulders. He took aim and launched the tail downwards, ramming his stinger between her shoulder blades.

But the stinger speared straight through and erupted between the girl's breasts, shooting its venom out onto the ground. Elaine's spine cracked, and her face froze in a silent wide-eyed scream.

The scorpion withdrew its stinger and dropped Elaine onto the sand. Now half paralyzed, the girl gasped rapidly, shaking in frail spasms.

The Bull mistook Elaine's stillness as the work of his venom, and it would have been far more merciful had that been the case. Elaine had absorbed no venom at all and was still very much alive.

Ready to feast, the Bull cruelly shoved his prey over. He extended his hideous jaws and re-gripped Elaine – right pincher clamping her chest and left pincher clenching her hips. Bending Elaine into an arc, the scorpion lifted her to its oral cavity.

The beast's jaws explored the prey, oozing digestive enzymes onto Elaine's abdomen. On contact with the fluid, the top layer of the girl's skin began to fizz and blister.

Her face fixed in an expression of horror, Elaine was fully aware of what was happening.

The Bull spread its jaws wide, opening their serrated bottom claws. He stabbed them into Elaine's tummy and tore her open. The girl's body jerked. And, as the beast raked up two jaws full of entrails, Elaine let loose an agonizing scream – a lasting, ear-splitting wail that echoed to every corner of the park.

The Bull plunged its jaws back in for more, and Elaine jerked again – her blood cascading onto the sand.

The girl's brain flooded with endorphins to block the pain.

Elaine's head pivoted limply about her neck. She stared deep into the infinity of stars above and asked, *Hesus ko, why?!*

But there was no answer. There was only a sense of the stars brightening and drawing Elaine's spirit towards them.

Tears gushed from her eyes and, gasping, she slid into shock.

The Bull polished off Elaine's lower torso then turned her – such that her legs were underneath its head and her bosom just below its jaws. He slathered her chest with enzymes then rapaciously shoveled up the melting flesh.

Beneath her bare ribcage, Elaine's lungs twitched, and her heart beat fitfully – trying, in vain, to circulate the remaining blood. The Bull's jaws grabbed Elaine's sternum and snapped it.

Blood spattered onto the girl's face and, as the life faded from Elaine's eyes, her final gasps grew into a death rattle.

The Bull's jaws pried open Elaine's ribcage, covered her heart and lungs with fluid, then clawed into the organs and yanked them up.

Sensing the quivering meat in his oral cavity, the Bull Scorpion was gratified – pleased with this odd new prey that he and his scouts had discovered. No outer shells. Just succulent flesh wrapped around thin, rigid sticks. And they bore more meat than any other creature they'd ever hunted! This new world promised a satisfying future.

As he continued to feast, the Bull's gray translucent joints turned a deep dark red.

▶ Back at the campgrounds, the number of scorpions was beginning to thin.

Gary and David peered out from their van.

Patrick, Tom, Yoli, and Billy looked out from the Winnebago's windows.

The scout finally moved away from the Johnson's Silverstream. Inside, Jim and Anne were seated on their small sofa – Jim solemnly holding a weeping Anne.

Al, Dan, Linda, and the Stewarts stared through Al's large living room window.

▶ The scorpions that remained were finishing their meals.

Mitch's scorpion had rendered him to mush.

Kathy's scorpion was scraping muscle from a severed leg. There was little left of the girl that anyone would have even recognized.

By the Reyes trailer, the remaining scout was raking the flesh from Michael's left arm. Once done, it dropped the bone to the ground to join the rest of Michael's bloody disjointed skeleton.

On the trail, the Bull Scorpion had inverted Elaine's body – its jaws now filleting her hips.

The girl's lifeless head and arms dangled upside down and brushed the ground – her eyes frozen-open in a straight-out death-stare. Blood and digestive fluid splattered down past her broken, empty ribcage.

The Bull's pinchers tugged on Elaine's thighs and tore away her legs. Her head, arms, and upper skeleton fell to the ground – with her gold cross landing face up in the sand by her neck.

The scorpion sucked the girl's hips half-way into its slavering oral cavity. Its jaws stripped away the remaining meat – lacerating Elaine's butterfly. And, seconds later, spewing acid, the beast spat out the hipbone.

Landing with a thud next to the girl's head, the pelvis splattered blood everywhere – burying Elaine's cross in a river of sandy red ooze.

The Bull stepped back to take stock of the remains. He set Elaine's right leg on the ground and then grasped her left leg with both pinchers. The monster raised the thigh to his jaws, slathered it in enzymes, and continued his meal.

On the ground below, tiny scavenging ants began crawling all over Elaine's ribs, arms, and face – even into her glassy, wide-open eyes.

▶ Four miles to the west, Steve's smashed Harley rested below the outcropping of inclined rocks.

Impatient, the scorpion that had pursued Jennie moved away from the crevasse and joined the monster devouring Steve. It squabbled with his brother over the boy's remains and, ultimately, tore a leg away for itself.

Lying on the floor of the stone alcove, Jennie remained unconscious – safe and breathing normally. She moved slightly, moaned a bit, and tried to lift her head. But she plopped back onto the sand and lapsed into sleep.

▶ At the Desert Rocks campgrounds, the few remaining scorpions each grabbed a scrap of prey and skittered off. Through their windows, the remaining campers watched them leave.

The first wave had ended.

PART THREE

Chapter 15

▶ Desert Rocks was now still.

Inside Al's living room, Margaret sat on the sofa, cuddling Tiffani. Frank joined her. Dan, Linda, and Al were scanning the campgrounds from the windows.

Tom yelled from one of the Winnebago's windows, "Dan! Al!"

Dan opened Al's front dining room window to answer. "Tom?!"

"I think they've gone. Everyone alright over there?"

"Those of us here!" said Dan, glaring at Frank. He turned back to Tom. "You guys?"

"Yoli 'n Billy freaked ... but Pat's nerves are steel!"

That gave Dan a nervous chuckle. "How's Jennie?"

Inside the Winnebago, Patrick grabbed Tom's shoulder and shook his head. Alarmed, he pointed at Al's house. "She told me she was joining Mom 'n Dad."

Tom turned and shouted back at Dan. "Dan?! Isn't Jennie with you?!"

Dan froze.

Panicking, Linda crossed to Dan. "Oh, no!"

Frank rose from the sofa and took a few steps forward. "Wait. She the girl with the punk red hair?"

Desperate, Dan confronted Frank. "Where is she?"

"With that biker-dude. They rode outta here an hour ago."

Dan glared at Frank. "What?!"

"I didn't know she was *your* kid. I thought she'd come with him."

"I'm gonna end up killing someone, yet!" Fuming, Dan grabbed his rifle. "Which way?"

"West, but–"

"West?!" interrupted Al. "He *can't* get through that way!" Al turned to face Dan. "For sure, he's stuck in powder or broken-down."

Dan crossed to the front door and yanked it open.

90

He strode onto Al's front porch and scanned the area. It appeared safe. Dan looked over at the Winnie and shouted, "Tom!"

Tom cautiously stepped out of the RV, rifle in hand. "I see ya, buddy!" He moved forward.

Dan stepped off the porch.

On pins and needles, they slowly and carefully approached one another – glancing around as they advanced, with their rifles at the ready. But the campgrounds were now still – no sign of the monsters. Dan and Tom met inside the picnic area, looked at each other, and exhaled in relief.

▶ Dan slowly drove Al's Land-Ranger towards the northwest end of the campgrounds. Tom, Al, and Frank were walking alongside – Frank nervously leading.

Frank stopped and pointed forward. "Here!"

Dan revved the Land-Ranger's engine and hit a switch. The vehicle's top floodlights went on, and the terrain lit up. The tracks left by Steve's Harley were now plain as day.

"There!" exclaimed Frank. "Now, get me back inside!"

"You just wait here a second," growled Tom, who then turned to Dan. "Sure you wanna do this?"

Dan silently nodded then switched on the dashboard's GPS unit, which displayed a topographical map. He turned to look back at Al, who was fixing an extra container of gasoline to the rear door. "Can this buggy handle it?"

"It's one of the few that can," responded Al. He closed the rear door and joined Tom and Frank.

"Watch out, Dan," cautioned Tom. "From what I just saw of the Reyes' trailer, those monsters are learning to tear into anything."

Frank grew more nervous. "Then, if ... if they come back, we need all the protection we can get."

Dan paused a moment in thought. "Al, didn't I see a ton of chicken wire in your shed?"

"Yeah."

"Okay. Pull everyone's vehicle 'round your house, then stake-down a fence outside of that." Dan looked up at Tom. "And *then*, have Pat 'n Linda rig my generator to it."

Tom brightened. "A 'lectric fence?"

"There's enough wire to handle it," confirmed Al.

"Then you'd better hurry up." Dan smiled at them and threw the Land-Ranger into drive.

Al patted Dan on the shoulder. "Good luck."

Dan nodded his thanks and, following the Harley's tracks, plowed the Land-Ranger into the terrain.

▶ Tom and David were inspecting Al's roof. No scorpions. David grabbed the binoculars and assumed the lookout post.

Tom headed towards the ladder. "Looks clear. You be alright?"

"No problem."

Tom began to descend. "Well, we've got a bright full moon, so keep an eye peeled."

"You can count on it!"

▶ Linda started the Winnebago's engine and turned on the headlights. Gary fired up his van and hit his lights as well. Jim followed suit in his Volvo.

Tom finished checking the hitch on the Reyes' pickup truck and trailer. Then, as Tom stood guard, Al started the pickup. Once he saw that Al was successfully moving the rig, Tom ran off towards Al's house. He could hear all of the vehicles running.

Frank backed the super coach out of his campsite. Anne drove Mitch's Mustang away from his collapsed tent. Yoli pulled out her van.

With Tom directing, everyone moved all of the vans and vehicles into a wide, nearly perfect circle around Al's house, shed, and yard. It almost looked like a wagon train preparing to ward-off the Apaches, but with plenty of space between each vehicle.

Chapter 16

► Linda stood just outside of the Winnebago, filling her generator with gasoline. Tom, rifle in hand, was standing guard not far from her. After locking the fuel cap, Linda fired up the unit.

Inside the Winnie, Patrick, Billy, and Anne were seated around Patrick's computer. The light fixtures went on, and a small wireless printer, which Patrick had placed near them, beeped.

They heard Linda shout from outside, "You've got an hour!"

Patrick yelled back his thanks and powered the laptop. As it booted, he fished through a plastic container and pulled out a thumb drive.

Billy gawked at the drive's hand-scrawled label. "Wikipedia?! You can download the whole site?!"

As he shoved the drive into the USB port, Patrick nodded. "Uh-huh. Did it just before we left home ... *in case* I got bored during the drive."

Wiki's home screen appeared. Patrick typed "scorpion" into the search blank and hit enter. The screen redrew into a detailed color image with text.

Anne's eyes lit up. "Well, we're lucky you *did!*"

Patrick scrolled through the text, blocking it off, then sent it to the printer.

► Al, Tom, Gary, and Frank stepped out of the shed. Heading for the edge of the fortress, they pushed a pair of wheelbarrows containing fence stakes, mallets, and two huge bails of chicken wire.

Together, Frank and Tom wrestled with the heaviest wheelbarrow while Gary slid the lighter one forward. Walking beside them, Al carried a shotgun and a small box.

Frank, straining from the real work, barked at Tom. "Well, so much for your *mountain lions!*"

"Oh ... I agree," acknowledged Tom. "But who could've seen *this* comin'?"

Frank shook his head. "Just tell me," he nodded at the chicken wire, "how's this fence gonna protect us?

"Hey, look," interrupted Gary, "I saw our bullets *burn* them. ... We *combine* our rifle-fire, we can bring one down."

"It's worth a try," agreed Tom.

Al hefted his shotgun. "Yeah, and I'm lookin' forward to giving these a try." He lifted a box of 12-gauge *slugs*.

Tom didn't look at the box close enough. "Doubt shot'll do much good."

But Gary caught what Tom had missed. "Tom, those are *slugs*."

Al grinned wickedly. "Found a few boxfuls."

"All right!" Tom smiled. "Any more shotguns?

"Few more, buried in the shed. ... Rob 'n I always prefer–" He stopped himself, then solemnly proceeded. "...*preferred* the rifles."

"We'll check back later," replied Tom. "Slugs aren't dead-on from a distance, but–"

"Yeah," exclaimed Gary, "at close range, they'd–"

"*Splatter* those fuckers!" raged Al.

Frank gave them an incredulous stare. "You all crazy?! What if there's hundreds of 'em?! ... I say we get the hell out of here! The road *must*'ve been cleared by now!"

Al stared at him coldly. "Don't you think we'd 've seen the state police if it was?

"Hell! We've not even seen a chopper fly over!" added Gary.

And Tom knew the reason. "Hard as San Berdoo was hit, you can bet all rescue forces 'r still there ... and *will* be there for a long time."

▶ As Patrick scanned his computer screen, Anne and Billy skimmed the pages that had been printed so far.

Anne was amazed. "It says here that scorpions can be *frozen* for extended periods ... *and remain alive!"*

"Yikes!" gasped Billy.

"I've got something here on *social* arachnids," offered Patrick.

Billy nervously laughed. "Oh yeah, these guys are regular party animals, aren't they?"

But Patrick was serious and hit the print key. "No, really ... You ever hear of communal spiders? Instead of living alone, they share a large common web or nest. Can even have a social structure, like ... like ants."

"Would that include scorpions?" asked Anne.

Looking at his screen, Patrick nodded. "Some species."

▶ While David continued his lookout from Al's roof, Linda, Gary, Yoli, Frank, and Jim stood at equal intervals around Al's house. With Tom again directing them, they all moved equidistantly away from the house, about 18 feet past the circle of vehicles, and then paused.

Tom quickly checked their positions. "Looks good. Now, everyone, just stay put!"

Al carried a large bail of chicken wire over to Linda. He and Tom handed her the open end and started to unwind the bail while moving on to the next person.

▶ As she lay face-down in the stone alcove, Jennie began to slowly come to. She moaned softly then suddenly jerked her head up, gasping. Dazed, she tried to figure out where she was. It appeared to be safe.

Jennie recalled her slide down the rock and, after looking upward, now realized what had happened. She felt her ribs and limbs, making sure nothing was broken, then carefully rose to her feet.

Pausing to listen, Jennie heard no droning and began to climb upward – the rough edges of the rock wall providing adequate footholds.

Cautiously, she poked her head up from the crevasse and looked around. No scorpions. Jennie crawled out, took a few steps forward, and turned. As she looked down, a scream caught in her throat.

There, just a few feet away, lay the mushy, disjointed remains of Steve.

▶ Back at the Winnebago, Patrick, Billy, and Anne continued their research.

Patrick peered intently at his screen. "Think I've ID'd them!"

Billy and Anne moved to look over his shoulder.

"Under the prehistoric species, there was *Gigantoscorpio* and *Brontoscorpio*."

"You're kidding!" exclaimed Billy.

"No, look at this." Patrick punched up an artist's rendition of a formidable and familiar creature.

"Holy shit, that's it!"

Patrick hit Control-P, and the printer began to buzz again. "Brontoscorpio. Length, about *one meter?!*"

"*One meter?!*" gagged Billy.

Anne shook her head. "How 'bout *four times that!?*"

▶ Three miles to the West, Dan continued pushing through the desert in Al's Land-Ranger. Desperately searching for his daughter, his eyes burned into the terrain ahead.

▶ At the circle of RV's, Al was about half way around the outer perimeter when the first bail of chicken wire ran out. Tom arrived with a second bail. With pliers and brute force, they firmly twined the two ends together and then moved on.

▶ Now four miles West, Dan had to pause the Land-Ranger. He had lost Steve's tracks.

But at that instant, Dan heard Jennie screaming. He looked through the passenger window and flicked on a handheld spotlight. Its beam revealed Jennie on top of a narrow pinnacle with a hungry scout on the ground below her!

Dan fired the Land-Ranger forward. Grabbing the PA microphone, he yelled over its loudspeaker, "Jennie! Jennie!"

The monster stretched towards the girl but, with no place to get a foothold, it couldn't reach her. Jennie had paid heed to Steve's last words about the creatures' weight.

Sensing the Land-Ranger's vibrations, the scorpion paused.

Dan stopped close by. He killed his lights, yelled taunts at the monster, honked, and began running the Land-Ranger in a tight circle.

The creature turned and started towards him.

"That's it," Dan mumbled, "This way!" Over the loudspeaker, he yelled, "Jennie! When I have drawn him away, climb down! I will swing back for you! Got it?!"

Dan saw Jennie nodding and then headed the Land-Ranger away – the scorpion, as hoped, following. *Yeah, this way. This way, you son-of-a-bitch!* As the scorpion pursued him, Dan checked his rearview. *That's right, dimwit! Focus on me!* Dan accelerated ever so slightly.

Carefully, Jennie made her way down the rock tower.

Dan led the scorpion a good distance away and slowed to let the creature draw near. As he saw the creature closing in, Dan made a sudden sharp left turn. He hit his lights and swung back in the direction he'd come – racing towards Jennie at full speed.

Confused, the monster paused, turned to look at the SUV, then began chasing its taillights.

Dan braked the Land-Ranger by the rocks. Jennie dashed for the passenger door, and Dan flung it open. The girl jumped in, collapsing onto the seat.

Just as the scorpion grew near, Dan sped away. The monster halted, angrily grabbing at and stinging empty air. It took several steps back, to get a running start, then threw itself forward in pursuit.

▶ Inside the Winnebago, the knowledge gathered from the encyclopedia was as thorough as it would ever be.

As Billy and Anne handed him their print-outs, Patrick shut-down his laptop and looked up. "Thanks for helping. I wanna review everything you've checked off."

"And connect the dots?" asked Anne.

Patrick nodded. "We've culled a lot of good info."

Billy turned to Anne. "Then let's go help with the fence."

"Do it," smiled Patrick.

As Anne and Billy headed out, Patrick grabbed a battery-powered lantern that sat next to the printer. "Hey, Billy! Kill the generator, will ya?"

"No problem!"

"Thanks."

Alone under the lantern light, Patrick spread the pages out in front of him. He grabbed a pencil, leaned forward, and knitted his brows.

Chapter 17

▶ Unwinding the last of the chicken wire, Tom and Al came full circle back to Linda – completing a loose perimeter around *Fort Nishida*. Anne and Billy approached them, bearing wooden fence stakes, two mallets, a small construction stapler, and boxes of staples.

As Linda held both ends taut, Tom and Al wove a stake through each separate end of the fence.

"Leave just enough room between these posts so we can cram in some kind of insulation," advised Tom.

"I know what'll do," said Al. "Billy, can you grab the cushion off my porch recliner?"

"Yeah! Perfect!" Billy handed Tom a mallet then dashed off.

Tom pounded the stakes into the ground, and then Anne began stapling the chicken wire to the stakes.

"Fasten it high, from the top down," advised Tom. "But make sure the wire's at least a foot above the dirt. It can't *ever* touch the ground."

"Got it!" nodded Anne.

Another stake was slid into the next point, followed by pounding and stapling. They continued around the circle, planting stakes where every person stood holding the wire and at the points halfway between. Stake, pound, staple. Stake, pound, staple.

Al took over the hammering so that Tom and Linda could move the Montgomery's generator to the fence's juncture. Patrick joined them and began splicing a pair of jumper cables to a long, thick extension cord – preparing them for connection to the fence.

▶ A mile West of the park and with nothing visible behind them, Dan slowed the Land-Ranger to a halt. He checked the GPS display then turned to Jennie, sighed, and smiled. For a moment, they silently looked at one another. Tears flowed from Jenny's eyes, and the two embraced.

"Dad, they got Steve! The last thing he did was to save me. ... He just wanted to bring back help!"

Dan held Jennie tightly and kissed her forehead. "Don't worry, sweetheart. It's okay."

At that moment, there was a resounding hiss. The pursuing scorpion came over the hill in back of them and paused.

Jennie cried, "Oh, no!"

"Damn!" Dan threw the Land-Ranger into gear and floored it – the scorpion giving chase.

As they sped away, a second scorpion scurried out from behind a boulder and paused right in their path. Dan managed to steer around the monster, and it followed too. No sooner had Dan looked forward when two more beasts appeared in front of him.

Deftly evading them as well, Dan glanced back. "Christ! Tom better have that fence ready!"

▶ With Tom, Al, Linda, and Patrick preparing the generator, the others focused on completing the fence. Gary and Jim planted two more stakes. Anne stapled down the wire. And Yoli ran to each stake, double-checking the wire and posts for sturdiness.

On Al's rooftop, David maintained the lookout. He heard the Land-Ranger approaching in the distance and raised his binoculars. "Someone's coming!"

Everyone paused.

Tom yelled, "'zit Dan?"

Happily, David lowered his glasses. "Yes! It's the Land-Ranger!"

Patrick brightened, "Dad!"

But the sound of droning scorpions began to grow.

David raised the glasses again. "Oh God, no! There's a mob of them stingers after him!"

Anxious, Tom turned to Patrick. "Pat?"

"Just a second more," said the boy, feverishly wrapping electrician's tape around the cable splices.

Less than a quarter-mile west, Dan raced the Land-Ranger towards Desert Rocks – with five scorpions giving chase.

The last fence stake was shoved through the wire and pounded down. The wire was stapled on and checked.

"We're done!" shouted Gary.

Tom yelled, "Then stand clear!"

100

As everyone else moved back inside the circle, Patrick plugged the cord into the generator and handed the clamps to Linda. She crossed to Al and Tom, who stood at the fence juncture. Billy approached with the cushion from Al's recliner. They could hear Dan honking.

The Land-Ranger tore through the park's entranceway.

Through their windshield, Dan and Jennie saw the fence and the others. Dan spotted the juncture and made a beeline for it.

Tom and Al yanked up a post, opening the fence, and the Land-Ranger shot through.

Seven scorpions swarmed past the park entranceway, heading for the fence.

From Al's roof, David fired his rifle at the beasts.

As the Land-Ranger screeched to a halt, Al moved the fence stake back into position. Billy jammed the cushion between the two posts, and Tom pounded the stake back down.

Then Linda secured the electrical clamps onto each side of the juncture. She stepped back and yelled, "Clear the fence!"

Now, as a total of ten scorpions rushed forward, Patrick fired up the generator.

The two leading monsters hit the fence – and *ZAP!* They were repelled in a shower of sparks. The beasts hissed in pain. A third scorpion tried to grab the fence with his pincher and was jolted back.

Patrick and Linda watched in awe as sparks showered to the ground.

Another scorpion tried to push through but was repelled.

Carrying rifles, Gary, Yoli, Frank, and Jim scrambled out to equidistant defense positions.

Tom and Al smiled, relieved that the fence was working.

As Dan and Jennie stepped out of the Land-Ranger, Linda and Patrick greeted them with hugs. Dan turned to look at the scorpions and saw the fence working perfectly.

The Bull Scorpion had joined the fray and pushed his way past the scouts to the front. Being somewhat larger, he tried to step over the fence but, even for him, it was too high. The beast took a huge jolt and yanked himself back, hissing loudly!

Dan raised his hands in victory. "Yes!"

Two more scorpions tried to breach the fence and were repelled. Everyone and every *thing* paused.
Standoff!

Chapter 18

▶ More scorpions had joined the others and, now, about twenty of the beasts had *Fort Nishida* surrounded. The electric fence, with Linda intermittently topping the generator's gas tank, was doing its job – effectively holding the creatures at bay.

On Al's front porch, Patrick, Billy, and Jennie were preparing Billy's toy helicopter for flight – intending to hover it above the monsters to beam back video for a head count.

The adults remained armed with rifles. Al, Linda, Yoli, and Frank maintained static posts between the vehicles – while Dan, Tom, Gary, and David warily patrolled the zone between the fence and the circled RV's.

Between Dan and Tom, another scorpion rushed the fence and was repelled.

As Dan walked past, Al growled, "Wish I could blast 'em with my slugs."

"Can't risk damaging the fence," cautioned Dan.

"Yeah," added Tom, "stick with the rifles for now."

Al grimly nodded. "For now."

Linda and Yoli stood not far from each other, cringing at the sight of the beasts.

"Jeez! They *are* hideous," stressed Linda.

Yoli nodded. "That stench turns my stomach!"

"Yecch," agreed Linda, "like vinegar and spoilt pork!"

At that moment, Margaret yelled from the super coach, "Frank! Frank, come here! Now!"

As Frank sighed and headed to his RV, Billy's model helicopter buzzed over his head and rose to cross the fence.

Jennie paced anxiously behind Billy and Patrick, who stood on Al's front porch and looked at the remote-control's video monitor. As Billy flew his helicopter slowly above the monsters, Patrick began taking his head count. But the buzz of the little chopper began to agitate the beasts. They sporadically reached up and tried to grab it.

"Billy," exclaimed Jennie, "don't piss them off!"

▶ Margaret was in a panic. The moment Frank entered his coach, she lit into him.

"You said the road 'd be clear by now! Why aren't you getting us out of here?!"

"Relax, Margaret. We're holding them off." Frank sighed in annoyance. "Now I need to get back out there." He headed for the door. "Help'll arrive eventually."

"*What* help?! Who even *knows* we're here?"

That stopped Frank cold in his tracks.

"For God's sake, Frank, those things are out to get us all! That generator won't run forever!"

Frank turned to face the front of the coach.

Margaret raged on, "You want us to end up like those stupid Flips?! We're people, damn it, not part of the fucking food chain!"

Determined, Frank started towards the front of the coach – Margaret hovering over his back.

Chapter 19

▶ The toy helicopter slowly cruised above the scorpions, just out of their reach.

Looking at the control unit's video screen, Patrick managed to get a fair count of the beasts. But he *was* finding it difficult to tell them apart, save for the Bull Scorpion.

Patrick noted that the Bull was a bit larger, and he pointed at the screen. "Bet ya he's their leader."

Billy hovered his chopper over the Bull. Eyes glued to the screen, Patrick and Billy saw the beast reach up towards the copter.

Patrick barked, "Quick, pull up!"

Though he couldn't seize it, the Bull was able to thwack the toy chopper and knock it back into the Fort. It hit the side of the Johnson's Silverstream and fell.

"Nuts!" Billy dashed off the porch.

Jennie shouted, "Wait!"

"Billy, just let it go!" yelled Patrick.

But Billy bolted for the copter.

While patrolling the fence, David had seen Billy's chopper fall to the ground. He was lifting it as the boy approached.

David smiled and handed the toy to Billy. "It'll be fine. We'll fix that blade later."

"Thanks."

As Billy took the chopper in hand, he and David heard one of the vehicles starting. They looked up in surprise.

Frank's headlights flashed on, and the super coach started pulling into the space between the vehicles and the fence. Dan, Al, David, Billy, and Tom ran towards the big RV, waving their arms and shouting. But it was too late. The super coach accelerated.

Frank clenched the steering wheel, glowering.

And Margaret, her mouth at Frank's ear, egged him on. "Faster!"

Frank hit his brights. He saw the scorpions fleeing the light and, smiling, straightened his steering. *Finally, in control!*

The super coach crashed through the fence, sparks flying everywhere. A whole section of the chicken wire untwisted and broke away. Dan's generator shorted and burst into flames.

With part of the fence caught in its front fender, the super coach rumbled on.

The droning Bull Scorpion charged past the downed fence – five of his scouts following.

"Everyone, head for the house!" yelled Dan.

The first scorpions impulsively ran outside the circle of RVs, which bought the people a few precious seconds. But the Bull then turned inward. With the beast charging straight between them, David and Billy were forced to split up. David ducked behind the Land-Ranger, and the Bull veered off in pursuit of Billy.

Thinking quickly, the boy swerved around Al's shed and crouched beside a crate. With Billy out of sight, the Bull paused a moment to look about but was soon lured away by the others racing for cover.

The remaining scorpions now rushed in.

David passed the Johnson's Silverstream. He noticed Anne, frozen in fear, standing outside her door. "Anne, get to the house! I'll cover you!" David climbed onto the adjacent pickup truck and lifted his rifle, but Anne hesitated.

In the next second, Jim dashed up and grabbed Anne's hand. "Come on, girl! Let's git!"

As the Johnson's fled, David caught a scout trying to dash past in pursuit. He fired his rifle. But the ravenous beast turned around. It reached up, dragged David to the ground, and skewered him.

▶ Breathing down Frank's neck, Margaret pointed ahead. "There's the entrance! Faster!"

Frank made a hard turn towards the gate and floored the accelerator.

As the super coach lurched forward, the chicken wire fell from the fender into the RV's front wheel and began winding into its axle.

Frank tried to straighten his steering, but it was frozen. With the speeding coach still turning, Frank looked down at the wheel. "What the...?!"

106

Alarmed, Margaret peered through the windshield. *"FRANK!"*
He looked up and slammed the brakes.

With a screech, the super coach rolled up the side of a huge sloped rock and tipped onto its left side – the windshield cracking into a thousand pieces.

▶ After several scorpions scurried past him, Billy stood the crate on end and, still grasping his toy chopper, climbed onto the shed's roof.

Dan and Linda held Al's front door open as everyone finished scrambling in. Then, as the Bull and a scout charged the porch, Dan yanked Linda inside and slammed the door.

Al, Tom, Gary, and Dan scrambled to secure the windows and doors while the others huddled in the center of the living room.

Scanning the room, Yoli stepped forward. "Billy? Billy?!"

▶ Two scorpions approached the overturned super coach. Sensing movement beyond the shattered windshield, they used their pinchers to begin punching through the safety glass.

Frank grabbed his rifle and rallied Margaret and Tiffani, who were bruised and disoriented. "This way!"

As Tiffani grabbed her doll, Frank tipped their dislodged mini-fridge to use as a step. He stood on the fridge and threw open the side door above them.

Frank stuck his head up – making sure it was safe – then climbed out and lifted Tiffani. At that moment, one of the scorpions pushed through the windshield into the coach. And, as it made a beeline for Margaret, Frank yanked her up in the nick of time.

Standing on the RV's side, they crossed to its edge. And just as the second scorpion crawled up in back of them, the Stewarts jumped off.

They hit the ground and started to break for Al's house. Tiffani's right leg, though, was still in pain, and she stumbled. Frank dropped his rifle to lift her – but with the second scorpion hitting the ground behind them, they had to scram.

▶ Yoli was freaking out. "Billy?!" She couldn't find him anywhere in Al's house.

Tom anxiously searched as well. "Billy?!"

Abruptly, Patrick called from Al's kitchen. "He's safe!"

From the dining room, Tom, Yoli, and Dan entered the kitchen to find Patrick peering out the window.

He pointed. "They don't see him!"

"Oh my God!" cried Yoli.

Through the window, they could see Billy lying quietly on the roof of Al's shed – clutching his toy copter. Below him, two scouts crept past, unaware of his presence.

And Billy – from *his* vantage point – could see the Stewarts, a good distance away, fleeing towards the house.

▶ Carrying Tiffani, Frank ran alongside Margaret.

Looking back from Frank's arms, Tiffani could see the pursuing scorpion closing in. "Daddy, faster!" Terrified, she began to cry and kick.

"Tiffani, *stop!*" barked Frank.

Her thrashing caused him to drop her. She hit the ground, and Frank grabbed her arm. He dragged her, trying to pick her back up. But the scorpion overtook them. With its left pincher, the beast seized the child.

Tiffani screamed!

Margaret turned. Aghast, she raced back.

As Frank struggled to hold on to Tiffani, Margaret joined him. The scorpion tugged. Frank and Margaret strained. But the scorpion yanked harder and plucked Tiffani from their grasp.

The beast lifted the screaming child towards its serrated jaws.

"*MOMMY!*"

Margaret rushed the beast.

"Margaret!" yelled Frank as he jerked his wife back – the beast's right pincher just missing her.

But maternal instinct trampled Margaret's fear. She fought. "*Let go of me!*"

The scorpion shoved Tiffani's head into its oral cavity. Acid covering her face, the child shrieked. And with a deft swipe of the beast's jaws, Tiffani's scream ceased with a *scrunch!*

Her doll hit the ground – its head breaking off.

Blood sprayed onto Frank and Margaret.

"*NO!*" Margaret still struggled.

"Margaret!" Frank pulled her back further.

"*TIFFANI!*" Margaret froze.

"She's gone!"

But no sooner did Frank yank Margaret around than they were faced with a second scorpion coming straight for them.

In shock, Margaret could barely mumble, "My baby!"

"Margaret! Move!"

Her grief swelling, she trembled. "My baby!"

Frank glared at the scorpion then back at Margaret. His angst peaking, Frank yelled, "*GOD DAMN IT!*" He shoved his wife directly at the beast and ran off.

The instant the monster seized her, Margaret snapped to. She screamed and managed to break free – but only for a moment. The creature shot forward and grabbed her again.

"Frank! *OH GOD!*"

But Frank just ran on – not even glancing back.

"*FRANK!*"

The scorpion whipped its tail forward, and the stinger shot through Margaret's skull – splashing her brain, like a ripe melon, onto the ground.

From the shed's roof, Billy had witnessed it all. Silently, he wept for Tiffani.

▶ Berserk, Frank charged forward – running past the circle of vehicles towards Al's porch. "Help!"

With his eyes focused solely on the front door, Frank didn't see the scorpions waiting in the shadows.

Through the living room window, Linda, Jennie, Al, Jim, Anne, and Gary clearly saw Frank approaching – though, knowing that the house was surrounded, Al could only shake his head.

Frank neared the porch. "*Open up!*"

When he hit the stairs, a scorpion shot out from under the porch and seized his ankle. Frank screamed as the beast dragged him back into the yard! Another scorpion fell onto Frank from the roof.

"*Help me!*"

Two more scouts joined the fray.

"*SOMEBODY!*"

The four beasts squabbled over Frank, each one tugging a limb. And the commotion attracted the Bull and more scouts.

"PLEASE!"

The monsters sunk their pinchers into him and pulled harder. With his muscles stretching beyond their limits, Frank felt his bones wrenched from their sockets. His ligaments tore, and he wailed in pain.

All at once, the scorpions yanked. With a final agonizing scream, Frank was ripped apart – his entrails streaming – right before everyone's eyes!

As Linda, Jennie, and Anne cried out in horror, Al whipped the curtains shut to hide the grisly sight.

▶ Tom, Yoli, Dan, and Patrick had remained in the kitchen to watch Billy.

Tom quietly opened the window to shout through the screen at him. "Billy! Billy. We see you. Just stay there. Don't move or make a sound!"

From the shed's roof, Billy looked at his father and silently nodded.

Tom pressed against the window-screen, "We'll try to–"

Suddenly, two pinchers lunged at the window and tore into the screen. As Tom pulled back, a scout yanked out the entire window frame and began to crawl through.

Dan, Patrick, Tom, and Yoli flew into the dining room. They slammed the door and shoved over a heavy cabinet as a blockade.

In the kitchen, the scorpion tried pushing on the door, but it wouldn't budge. After a few tries, the beast simply backed up and patiently stared at the door – waiting.

Billy couldn't help but see the Stewarts being devoured below him. The distant scorpion was making a quick snack of Tiffani. A few yards away, the second scorpion was savagely shredding Margaret's torso. And, in Al's front yard, a total of seven scorpions fiercely devoured the frayed fragments of what had, moments before, been Frank.

Horrified, Billy buried his face on his arm – but his motion nearly caused him to slip. He swiftly grabbed the roof's apex – *Whew!* – and took a deep breath.

Chapter 20

▶ Everyone was spread across Al's living room and connected dining room. Tom and Yoli anxiously watched Billy from a side window. Patrick was seated near them at the dining room table. And peering over Patrick's shoulder, Dan and Linda studied his Wikipedia print-outs.

Patrick explained, "We can only guess, of course. But they must have been underground. And got trapped by some freak of nature that ... well ... *froze* them."

"For millions of years?" Linda asked.

"Literally," nodded Patrick, "for eons."

"And the recent quakes freed them," surmised Dan.

"Here," Patrick lifted an illustration he'd printed, "an artist's rendering based on fossils. Look familiar?"

"*I'll* say!" Dan grabbed the page for a closer look.

While they focused on the image, Al gingerly weaved his way from the living room into the hallway.

▶ Rifle in hand, Al entered his bedroom and quietly shut the door. He tossed the Marlin onto his bed.

His energy dropping, Al gazed at the picture frames resting across the dresser top. He placed his hand on the far left one – a photo of Robert taken at his graduation.

Slowly, Al moved his hand across the others: A double frame holding portraits of Robert and Lauri. Another frame with a shot of them laughing and hugging. A family shot of a young Al with his much younger wife, Tomoko, and a baby Robert. And finally, a portrait of Tomoko in her later years.

Tears welled up in Al's eyes. He lifted his wife's portrait and whispered, "If only you were here, Tomie, I ... I would be able to go on."

▶ With a sigh, Dan tossed the illustration back onto the dining room table.

Patrick was recapping what he'd surmised before, "So we know that they're prehistoric, mostly nocturnal, and *communal*.

"Communal?" Linda realized, "Then, they *must–*"

"Yes!" exclaimed Dan, "... have a common *nest* somewhere!"

▶ Returning Tomoko's picture to his bedroom dresser, Al glanced up at the Samurai sword hanging on the wall. He took it down and reverently pulled the katana several inches from its sheath. Al looked at its keen edge – an edge that he had always, honoring tradition, kept super sharp. And, as he lingered on the blade, his eyes flared. Anger began to swell deep inside him, and Al slammed the sword back into its case.

He crossed to his desk, where a shotgun and box of slugs awaited. After placing his sword on the desktop, Al lifted the shotgun, pumped out the remaining shot, and began loading the gun with slugs.

▶ With dawn approaching, the sky began to lighten.

The Bull Scorpion crossed in front of Al's house and emitted a short drone – calling to his scouts. The scorpions all began to stir and answered the Bull with short bursts of their own.

Tom, Patrick, and Dan crossed to look back out the dining room windows.

On the shed's roof, Billy – half asleep – stirred from the droning. He moved slightly and started to slip downward. Startled, the boy struggled to stop himself – but he'd slid well below the top and, in his scramble, inadvertently released the toy copter. The chopper slid – singing down the corrugated metal – and hit the ground.

Hearing the crunch, the Bull Scorpion whipped around to see Billy inching down the roof. As the beast crept towards him, Billy spread his limbs – trying futilely to break his slide.

From the dining room window, Tom saw what was happening and freaked. "No!"

Yoli screamed.

Tom rushed for the front door. "Oh God, *NO!*"

And Dan dashed after him. "Tom!"

Thinking fast, Gary crossed the living room and seized Al's coat rack. Jim grabbed his rifle and moved behind Gary.

Tom clasped the door, but no sooner did he start to open it than a pincher shot inside. As Dan yanked Tom back to safety, Gary shoved the claw back with the coat rack, and Jim fired his rifle straight into the scout's eyes. The beast reared back, and Anne and Jennie slammed the door.

Slapping his hands to his forehead, Tom ran back into the dining room, "I'm sorry, I'm sorry," then screamed out the window, "Billy!"

As Al attached the Samurai sword to his belt, he could see Billy and the Bull Scorpion from his bedroom window.

The Bull reached upward.

Panicking, Billy scrambled. "Help!" But his motion caused him to slide faster – right into the beast's clutches. *"HELP ME!"*

Once seized, Billy fought madly.

The Bull raised its stinger.

Yet, as the monster yanked the struggling boy around, it swung Billy towards the shed – smacking his head against the wall and knocking him out.

Billy went limp, and the beast paused – presuming its prey had succumbed.

With its appetite already sated, the Bull didn't harm the boy. Instead, it simply held onto him – a meal to carry back to his young.

In the dining room, Yoli cried out and buried her face in Tom's chest.

Patrick had watched carefully, though. "It didn't sting him!"

Tom clutched at the window. *"Dios mio!* Holding him for later?!"

"Yeah," Patrick acknowledged, "but it buys him time."

Dan's eyes lit up, the spark of a plan hitting him.

The Bull resumed droning, and the scouts began to gather around him.

Patrick could hear the scorpion in the kitchen crawling back outside, and they all saw it approaching the Bull.

"For sure, that big one's *calling* them," observed Dan.

"Oh no!" cried Yoli.

Dan faced her and Tom. "No ... wait."

"Yeah, with the sky lightening," inserted Patrick, "they'll be starting back for their lair."

"Exactly," nodded Dan, "and that gives us a chance to save Billy!"

Tom brightened, "You're right!"

Yoli looked up in hope.

With the scouts gathered around him, the Bull raised Billy like a trophy and droned in triumph.

Al crawled out of his bedroom window, shotgun in hand, and quietly slid the window shut. He checked his sword then moved forward.

The scorpions began leaving the campgrounds – the Bull leading the way. And following them at a guarded distance, stealthy as a cat, was Al.

Peering through the dining room window, Dan and Tom saw Al tracking the monsters. They looked at each other for a moment then broke into action.

Tom grabbed his rifle and a box of ammo and headed towards the front door. He carefully checked before opening it and then headed out.

As Dan grabbed his rifle and ammo, he called, "Linda, Jim, Gary!" and pointed to Al's gun rack. "Each of you take a rifle and keep guard here."

Linda asked, "Dan?! What are you–"

"We've *got* to find their nest," answered Dan as he headed for the door.

▶ As the pre-dawn sky grew lighter, the scorpions scuttled rapidly across the desert – Al in relentless pursuit.

Tom was too far behind to see them in the rocky terrain, and he feared that he'd lost Al's tracks. Within moments, though, he came upon them again and paused.

Panting, Dan caught up to Tom, who gestured at the tracks. "Gotta be this way."

Dan nodded, and the two men moved on.

▶ Al trudged to the top of a hill and halted beneath a transmission tower. Looking down, he saw the monsters nearing the fissure.

The Bull Scorpion paused at the opening, waiting for all of his scouts to enter. Then, with Billy still in its clutches, the Bull followed them inside.

Al headed down the hill in pursuit – the morning sun rising in back of him.

Chapter 21

▶ The scorpions crawled deep into the cavern, which was now faintly lit by luminous moss – a primal *goblin gold* that had glowed back to life after the interior ice had melted.

Slowly, Billy began to regain consciousness. As he opened his eyes, Billy realized that he was still in the grip of a pincher. He caught his voice and froze – reckoning that playing dead would keep him from being stung. And, as the Bull carried him further from the opening, Billy saw the sunlight fade.

To reach their nest, the scorpions had to pass through a large feeding den. It was there that the Bull halted. He droned loudly and set Billy on the ground. After seeing movement behind the rocks, the Bull deemed his job done and exited through an opposing tunnel that led to the nest.

Billy heard a soft clicking and lifted his head to behold a few three-foot-long scorpions scuttling from the shadows straight at him. Horrified, he scrambled to his feet then dashed away.

The young scorpions paused in surprise, hissed, and gave chase.

▶ Al entered the fissure and prowled deep into the cavern, noting that the classic limestone formations were erratically laced with veins of black lava rock. *Caused, no doubt, by an ancient upheaval*, thought Al.

As he approached the edge of the feeding den, Al's foot hit something. He froze and looked down. Below him lay the upper skeleton of an earlier victim – face turned away, half of its skull exposed.

Trembling, Al bent closer and, with the tip of his shotgun, pushed over what was left of Lauri's face. The right eyeball was rolled back and withered inward. Patches of remaining flesh had turned bright green. Strands of bloodied blonde hair strung outward from the shattered cranium. And, below the skeletal neck, lay Lauri's broken necklace – its chain encrusted with dried brown blood.

Suddenly, a small centipede scurried out from the left eye socket – startling Al. He jumped back – his emotions veering from shock to rage. Al turned and ran deeper into the feeding den, calling, "Billy! ... BILLY!"

Not far away, the boy cried for help, and Al ran towards his voice.

He paused in the middle of the den and saw Billy, cornered by the three young scorpions. The boy had climbed to an elevated ledge and was swinging a human femur at the young monsters whenever they got close – smacking back their pinchers. The scorpions had been unable to gain sufficient foothold on the lava rock, and they couldn't quite reach Billy. But neither could Billy get away.

With a bloodcurdling yell, Al dashed forward – distracting the scorpions into going for him. "Billy, get down from there!" Al lifted his shotgun.

As the first young scorpion lurched at him, Al fired a slug and blew its head apart!

He pumped the shotgun.

The other two young scorpions charged.

Al fired again, splattering the second one's carapace. But as he reracked the gun, the third juvenile lunged forward and yanked it from his hands. With both pinchers, the beast snapped the shotgun in two.

Al now drew his sword and, while dodging the creature's stinger, hacked its right pincher clean off. He then dashed behind the little bastard, grabbed the top of its tail, and viciously gutted him. The young scorpion shrilled.

During all of this, Billy was able to climb down and inch his way towards the front tunnel.

Coming from the nest with a roaring hiss, a full-grown scout entered the den. Al looked up, and the scout turned to lay hold of what had gone down.

Billy stopped to look back. "Al!"

But, with his sword at the ready, Al glanced at Billy and screamed, *"GET OUTTA HERE!"*

Reluctantly, Billy obeyed.

Another hiss shot through the cavern, and Al pivoted. A second scout entered the den. But this one scurried off to the side, to be concealed by other rocks.

The first scout made a run at Al, and Al sliced into its pincher. For the first time, the beast felt pain.

As the creature backed up, a third scout entered the den and dashed at Al. Again, the man hacked into this one's pincher. But it tried grabbing him with its other claw – and, with a deft slash of his sword, Al cleaved the pincher in half.

Smarting, the third scout backed up and joined the first. They droned at each other. Never before had prey stung back. And it had just killed three of their young! But at this moment, from across the den, the droning of the second scout echoed over to them.

Billy paused part-way through the front tunnel to look back. He could see Al, and he did *not* want to leave him.

Together, the first and third scouts now moved slowly towards Al – backing him towards a boulder. And when Al pressed his back against the stone, without warning, the second scout shot up from behind and seized him by the shoulders.

Al yelled and thrust his sword upward – driving it into the second scout's carapace with a sickening *crunch!* In reflex, the creature whipped its stinger forward – straight into Al's chest.

Al screamed.

He and the scorpion both shook in convulsions – Al pushing his sword deeper into the monster's head as the beast pumped venom directly into his heart.

With the poison flooding his arteries, Al's vision swirled, and he promptly blacked out.

The first and third scorpions grabbed Al's legs. They began to tug. And the sword, which Al still clenched, slid out of the second scout's head.

In the front tunnel, Billy screamed, *"AL!"* He stumbled backwards, in tears, then fled for the fissure opening.

As the scorpions dragged him across the den, Al released his sword. It rested in the dust like a fallen monument.

The wounded scout staggered back from the boulder and collapsed – dead.

▶ Billy flew through the fissure opening into the warm morning sunlight.

As Dan and Tom broke the crest of the hill above, they saw Billy dashing madly towards them.

Tom shot forward. "Billy!"

"Dad!" The boy crashed into his father's arms, crying. "Dad! They killed Al!"

Tom hugged his boy.

"He saved me." Billy buried his head on Tom's shoulder and continued sobbing. "And now he's dead!"

Tightening his hug on Billy, Tom closed his eyes and hung his head in grief.

Dan approached and stooped to meet Billy at eye level. "Where, Billy? Where are they?"

Barely able to speak, the boy turned and pointed downward at the fissure. "There! Way down in there!"

As Tom did his best to comfort Billy, Dan stepped forward. He peered down at the crevasse, realizing that they had found the gateway to the scorpions' nest.

At that moment, Dan also realized he was hearing a faint hum – one coming from the power lines above him. He looked up at the nearest transmission tower and ran 20 yards uphill to gaze outward from its base. Like the others wired to it, this tower was one of a smaller class – only about 60 feet tall. Following the power lines off to the north, Dan's eyes saw a small distant substation – one that was nestled on a hillside and fed by lines from larger towers.

He looked back at the tower above him then hurried down to Tom and Billy.

"Tom," exclaimed Dan, pointing to the power lines with his thumb, "This grid's still *hot!*"

119

PART FOUR

Chapter 22

▶ "So it's clear that they've learned to tear into anything to get at us," stated Patrick. It was now about 8 am. Everyone was gathered just outside of Al's house by the back door, listening.

Yoli sat nearby in the back of Robert's Wrangler, hugging Billy tightly. Jennie and Anne stood just outside the vehicle in support – Jennie handing Billy a small bottle of Gatorade and Anne placing a comforting hand on Yoli's shoulder.

Dan, Tom, Jim, Patrick, and Linda stood together, inspecting the ripped-up kitchen window.

Tom lifted part of the frame, and it broke away. The wood was rotted. He shook his head. "And, for sure, *termite terrace* here ain't gonna shield us for another night."

The prospect unnerved Linda. "So what can we do?"

"Plenty," affirmed Dan, "but we've gotta act fast!"

▶ Dan, Tom, Gary, Patrick, and Jim entered Al's shed to raid his stockpiles. Patrick shoved cans of Sterno into a bag. Tom grabbed a few flare guns and boxes of aerial flares. Gary hoisted the last three shotguns onto his shoulder. Dan pulled down three large canisters of insecticide. And Jim snatched the remaining boxes of slugs and rifle cartridges.

Lastly, Dan yanked out a wooden crate he found under one of the metal shelves and pried it open. "My God! Al must've forgotten he had this!" Lying inside were ten Orion flare guns and two hundred aerial flares.

At the fallen Fort Nishida, Anne was in her Silverstream – going through their belongings – and happily came across a box of road flares. Linda unlocked an exterior side panel of the Winnebago and pulled out three reserve cans of gasoline. Inside, Jennie was rummaging through their kitchenette. As she opened the cabinet beneath the sink, her eyes lit up. There, fastened into a rear corner, stood five canisters of propane.

▶ Minutes later, Patrick pointed at the Stewarts' overturned super coach. Linda, Jennie, Billy, Gary, and Anne got his meaning and dashed towards it.

Within seconds, they were enthusiastically tearing apart its interior. Linda, Jennie, and Anne yanked the foam rubber from all the cushions. While ransacking a cabinet, Billy came across Frank's case of condoms. He unrolled one and blew it up like a balloon.

Gary was pulling memory foam from a bed mattress when he looked up and saw Billy. He laughed and lifted the condom box. "Hey! These are polyurethane, not latex. Hmm … I'll bet we could get away with–" Gary paused, smiling.

"We could get away with *what?*" laughed Billy.

Deep in thought, Gary smiled and responded only with a chuckle – keeping Billy in suspense.

"With *WHAT?!!!*"

▶ At the Hernandez campsite, Yoli rifled through their boxes – pulling out bags of charcoal briquettes and canisters of lighter fluid.

Gary stepped into her screen-house to ask, "Uh, Mrs. Hernandez? May I appropriate that large cooler of yours? Got a good tactical use for it."

Yoli smiled and pushed the cooler his way. "It's yours!"

▶ The picnic tables had become work stations for fabricating unique weapons, and everyone was busy.

On his crutches, Patrick hobbled past each table, nodding.

He joined Billy and Jennie at the first table, making fume bombs. Wearing rubber gloves, all three cut up chunks of foam rubber, buried charcoal briquettes and open cans of Sterno inside each chunk, then soaked all of the pieces in a bowl of insecticide. Next, they inserted each piece into a separate Baggie and ran a paper straw dampened in lighter fluid – to use as a fuse – from the Sterno through the twist-tied top of each bag.

At the second picnic table, Linda and Yoli used jars, gasoline, and rags to fashion a load of Molotov cocktails.

Dan and Tom had driven the Land-Ranger to the cable-laying site along Highway 18 and were loading the large coil of electric cable onto the bed of the Cal-Ed truck. Then, as Tom looked on, Dan slim-jimmed the truck's door open and hot-wired the ignition. After the truck started, Dan climbed behind the wheel, Tom returned to the Land-Ranger, and they both pulled away.

Back at Desert Rocks, Anne labored alone at the third picnic table – sorting through firewood and spray cans of insecticide. At the fourth table, Jim organized their collected fire power – taking stock of all the rifles, shotguns, shells, flare guns, and aerial flares they had. And finally, Gary sat at the fifth table, making *gas balloons* by filling Frank's condoms with gasoline, tying their tops, and then gingerly placing them in the Hernandez' large cooler.

▶ Upon returning to Desert Rocks, Dan disconnected Al's television antenna and carried it off. Likewise, Tom removed the antenna from the roof of the Stewart's super coach.

At the fifth picnic table, Gary had finished the balloons and was now filling several white trash bags with just enough gasoline to create a healthy explosion when ignited.

Dan and Tom worked with the steel antennae at the sixth picnic table. Paring them down, they created two electrodes – Dan making handling areas on the back end of each with foam rubber and electrician's tape.

At the perimeter of the fallen fort, Yoli, Billy, and Jim wound up all of the chicken wire while Anne and Jennie collected the fence stakes.

Linda, per Dan's instructions, removed the tools from the Cal-Ed truck and placed them on the back floor of Robert's Wrangler.

And just outside of Al's storage shed, Gary carved a pile of wooden poles into long deadly spikes while Tom carried off the finished ones to stow in the Land-Ranger.

▶ An hour later, the Land-Ranger and the Wrangler pulled up from a dirt trail to stop beside the small power substation – the one Dan had seen earlier from the fissure site. The substation itself was mainly a modest step-down transformer, caged inside a metal fence.

Each of the two SUVs contained one of the electrodes. The Land-Ranger additionally carried the large coil of power cable and

Gary's long spikes. The Wrangler also held the fence stakes, the hand tools, and two sizable coils of chicken wire.

As Tom and Gary stepped down from the Jeep, Dan exited the Land-Ranger with a sledgehammer. Jim and Anne stepped out of the Land-Ranger to stretch their legs, while Dan, Tom, and Gary approached the fence.

With a resounding thwack, Dan smashed the lock off the gate, and the three men pushed the fence open.

As they approached the control wall, Gary questioned, "Wouldn't it be easier if we just *blew up* the cave opening?"

Tom shook his head. "Man, it's a fissure! If we blast that entrance, the whole front end 'll crumble 'n open up right above!"

"*And*, if we're not thorough, those bastards 'll come back to feast on us all!" added Dan, his eyes scanning the control panel. He lifted a metal box and found a large metal switch.

Dan reached up and pulled the switch down to *off*.

Chapter 23

► The Wrangler and Land-Ranger were now parked at the fissure site, just beneath the tower. Dan, Tom, Gary, Jim, and Anne – each with a rifle slung over a shoulder – finished offloading their materials.

Once everything was spread across the ground, Tom climbed back into the Land-Ranger, hit the button that closed his tailgate, and started the engine.

"Hurry, man," said Dan. "We gotta have it all ready before sundown!"

"Don't worry. We'll be here."

For a moment, Dan watched Tom drive away, anxious about keeping on schedule. As the Land-Ranger disappeared over the hill, Dan peered up at the tower and shouted to Gary, Jim, and Anne. "Okay, folks! Let's boogie!"

Heading back to the campgrounds, Tom pressed the Land-Ranger over the rugged terrain as fast as he could. He frequently studied Al's GPS unit – plotting the quickest path for their return.

Half-way up the hill, about two hundred feet from the fissure itself, Jim and Anne began hammering down the fence posts – planting them in a semicircle that curved away from the opening. Meanwhile, Dan scaled the tower, carrying a short piece of cable and a large enclosed knife switch. He paused just below the tension lines and tied his cable to the metal. On the ground below, Gary crossed to the opposite side of the hill, carrying the first electrode. Using hefty stones, he fixed it into position near the first fence stake. Above, Dan disconnected one of the tension lines, and it fell to the ground.

► Near the top of the tower, just a few rungs below the power lines, Dan finished installing the knife switch. Below the tower, Gary was positioning the second electrode, and Jim and Anne were pounding the last of the fence-posts into position.

At Desert Rocks, Tom honked as he pulled the Land-Ranger into the campgrounds. Linda, Patrick, Jennie, Yoli, and Billy ran up – ready and waiting. They had the Reyes' pickup and the Cal-Ed truck packed and ready to go.

Tom was impressed. "All right!" He turned the Land-Ranger around and pulled next to the last several boxes of homemade weapons.

"What kept ya?" teased Patrick.

"Thank heavens you're all ready," responded Tom. "We've no time to waste!"

He punched open the Land-Ranger's tailgate, and everyone started to shove the boxes into its rear bed.

At the fissure site, Jim and Anne began stapling the chicken wire to the fence posts. Dan and Gary stood near the tower, holding the large coil of electrical cable. With the cable now connected to the downed power line, they loosely unwound the coil – in back of and above the fissure opening – crossing over to the first electrode. There, Dan cut the cable and started fastening it to the conductor.

Back at the campgrounds, Tom loaded the last box. Closing the tailgate, he shouted, "Let's move it!"

He and Patrick got into the Land-Ranger. Linda and Jennie entered the Cal-Ed truck. Yoli and Billy boarded the Reyes' pickup. With Tom in the lead, they pulled out and began grinding their way through the badlands.

As Jim and Anne finished stapling the chicken wire, Dan and Gary completed fastening the power cable to the first electrode.

Tom's convoy entered rockier terrain, and the Cal-Ed truck got stuck in a bed of soft dry sand. Linda tried rocking the truck back and forth, but the maneuver was no good. The tires simply dug deeper into the powder.

Along the fence, Jim and Anne began mounting the long spikes that Gary had carved earlier – pointed inward, like a medieval booby trap.

With Gary beside him, Dan finished connecting the second electrode to a line running up the side of the tower to the knife switch.

"Head on," Dan said to Gary. "I'll shoot up a flare when ready."

Gary nodded, "You got it!" He jumped into the Wrangler and drove away on the dirt service road.

127

With Linda still behind the steering wheel, Yoli, Tom, Jennie, and Billy tried pushing the Cal-Ed truck out of its trap. Linda aggressively worked the clutch and accelerator as the others strained. The rear wheels spun and stopped, but the plan didn't work. The truck was now hopelessly dug in.

"It's no use," declared Tom. "Come on."

They began moving the truck's contents into the remaining space in the Land-Ranger and the Reyes' pickup.

Pulling up in the Wrangler, Gary arrived at the power substation. He hopped to the ground and crossed to gaze down at the distant fissure site.

Jim and Anne continued mounting the spikes, at regular intervals, through the fence. Dan was back up on the tower, checking the connection on the knife switch.

At the stalled convoy, everyone finished moving the boxes, slammed their doors, and headed on – leaving the Cal-Ed truck stuck in the sand. Linda piloted the Land-Ranger. Yoli drove the Reyes' pickup. And Tom and Jennie walked alongside, bearing two small boxes that wouldn't fit. Trudging forward, the pickup scraped a rock on its underside but continued on.

Up on the tower, Dan backed away from the connected knife switch and faced the distant substation. He raised a flare gun above his head and fired.

Gary smiled as he saw the flare streaking across the sky. He dashed into the substation and switched the current back on.

With the lines humming again, Dan returned to the knife switch. He paused to look down at the Johnsons and shouted, "Move back! Move back!"

Jim and Anne placed the last spike at the end of the fence and backed away a safe distance. Dan looked down at both electrodes – strategically placed halfway up each side of the hill. *This had better work!* As he threw the switch, tiny sparks squirmed across its metal casing. And a powerful bright electric arc now danced between the conductors.

From his viewpoint at the substation, Gary was ecstatic on seeing the arc. "YES!" Clapping his hands, he jumped into the Wrangler and started back.

Thrilled, Jim and Anne gave Dan two thumbs up. He switched off the current and sighed in relief. At that very moment, Dan heard the Land-Ranger and the pickup's engines coming near, and he looked outward to see the vehicles appear over the opposite hill – Tom and Jennie walking alongside.

Dan descended the tower, pleased that all was going to plan. As Yoli and Linda stopped the vehicles above the fissure, Jim and Anne ran over to greet everyone.

On the dusty service road, Gary pulled the Wrangler up beneath the tower and jumped out, belting a fervent, "Fuckin' *A*, man!"

Dan hit the ground, put his arm around Gary, and pointed to the area contained by the fence. "Everyone! *Here* is where we plant the firetrap!"

▶ Shovels gashed into the sandy dirt.

Glancing at his wristwatch, Patrick kept an eye on the time while everyone else vigorously dug holes within the semicircle.

Then, Anne and Jennie braced the long pointed spikes by placing Al's wood dining chairs against the outside of the fence, sliding the spikes through the back of the chairs, and weighing them all down with hefty rocks.

Dan and Gary carefully planted the gasoline-filled plastic bags within each hole.

Billy dropped combustibles into other holes – paper, foam chunks, and dried out tumbleweeds.

Jim swung down a hoe, digging a small trench. He worked his way up the slope to the rear center of the fence. From Jim's main channel, Yoli and Linda hoed tributaries downward and off to the sides.

Billy tossed more shrubs on top of the holes and weighted them down with stones.

"'zit gonna work, Dan?" asked Tom.

With a determined glint in his eyes, Dan looked around at everyone's handiwork and nodded. "It's *got* to!"

Chapter 24

▶ The sun was getting low in the sky. Tom and Gary carried the large cooler, which was filled with the gas balloons, over to the tower. Dan and Linda were up near the top by the knife switch.

Dan fastened a safety harness around Linda and gave her a quick kiss. "You be alright up here?"

"I'll be fine. It's you and Tom we're worried about."

As Dan continued to instruct Linda on using the switch, Tom arrived just below them.

Dan held up his hand. "Hey, right there. Fifteen feet below the switch 'll be fine. Can't risk a spark hitting 'em."

"Right!" Tom threw a rope over one of the beams and began hoisting the cooler.

Just below, Gary climbed the tower and guided the cooler by hand – making sure it didn't snag anywhere on the metal.

On the ground, Anne and Jennie finished bracing their last spike.

Yoli, with a rifle and shotgun, positioned herself near the first electrode. Anne, rifle in hand, took her position near the second electrode.

Patrick and Jennie positioned themselves on the rock ledge above the fissure opening, lying on their stomachs and juggling two flare guns each. Billy joined them, lugging a box full of flares, and began loading their guns.

Jim and Gary stepped up to the top of the hill, just behind the center of the fence – both with flare guns wedged behind their belts. Gary also held a shotgun and Jim, a rifle. At their feet rested two boxes of Molotov cocktails and five metal buckets filled with gasoline.

With Dan's help, Tom securely tied the large cooler onto the corner of the tower.

▶ With the sun now close to setting, Dan and Tom took their positions in front of the fissure entrance. Each man carried a large pack on his back – stuffed with firewood, a small propane tank, road flares, and fume bombs. Each also had a shotgun strapped over his shoulder, a flare gun in his belt, and goggles and a respirator around his neck.

Dan reached back into his pack and withdrew a road flare.

"Well, partner?" said Tom as he switched on a flashlight and beamed it into the cavern.

Dan nodded. "Yeah. Into the depths of Hell." He ignited the flare and threw it into the cavern as far as he could.

They turned to look back at the others for a moment. Then each took a deep breath and headed in.

The men proceeded cautiously. Tom lit the immediate path with his flashlight. And Dan, after going in a ways, tossed ahead another road flare to light the surroundings.

Outside, the sun began to drop below the horizon and the moon began to rise.

Dan and Tom walked deeper into the cavern and entered the feeding den. As Dan tossed ahead a third flare, the eerie sound of droning scorpions rose from deep within the caverns.

"Listen," whispered Dan.

On edge, the two men stopped in their tracks.

"Hmm," nodded Tom. "Gettin' ready for their evening's hunt."

"Well ... what say we spoil it for 'em?!"

As he stepped forward, Dan looked down and paused. There, in the dust, was Al's sword. "Al," whispered Dan solemnly. He lifted the sword and secured it to his belt.

Following the sounds, the men entered the tunnel that led to the nest.

They carefully tread down the path for a few hundred feet, stepping around several large rocks. Perceiving the dim glow of the luminous moss on the tunnel wall, Tom killed his flashlight.

A cluster of large boulders sat at the far end of the tunnel. Past that, the two men could make out a larger cavern – the scorpions' principal nest.

Dan and Tom crept up to the boulders and cautiously peered over them – staring in dread at the Bull and the several scouts gathering around him.

"If hell-spawn was ever on earth ..." whispered Tom.

Placing his hand on Tom's shoulder, Dan whispered back, "Let's get this done with."

Moving back a bit to the opposite walls of the tunnel, Dan and Tom pulled off their backpacks. Behind several of the larger rocks, each man quickly built a wide pile of firewood, placing several fume bombs within. They doused the pyres with lighter fluid and firmly set a canister of propane on top of each – planting the bottom halves securely then topping the canisters with multiple spray cans of insecticide.

As Tom moved back to the cluster of boulders, Dan ran a ten-foot kerosene-soaked rope – a time-delay fuse – from his pyre.

Then Dan joined Tom beside the boulders, where they put on their goggles and respirators. They pulled out more fume-bombs, lit their fuses, and flung them as far into the nest as they could.

When the bombs landed, their smoky fumes repelled the nearest scorpions. The beasts scrambled back – deeper into the cavern.

Dan and Tom hurled several more fume bombs, landing them deep in an opening on the opposite wall. The smoke unfurled, causing more scorpions to scramble in distress.

As the men continued to lob in more bombs, the Bull Scorpion became agitated. He droned fiercely at his scouts, only to see them clutching at the air and colliding with each other.

"Time to light your stack!" called Dan.

And while Dan continued flinging fume-bombs, Tom returned to his pyre and put a match to its base.

Suddenly, a scout scrambled up on top of the boulders – startling Dan. It paused, calling to its brothers. Immediately, Dan fired a flare, which the monster dodged – though the burst of light made all the beasts freeze.

As Dan reloaded, Tom lifted his shotgun and fired a slug at the scout. The beast tumbled backwards – the top of its head blown off. And Dan ran over to ignite his long fuse.

The gun blast echoed throughout the caves and snared the Bull's attention.

Two more droning scorpions scrambled up onto the boulders. But when Tom blasted *their* heads off, the Bull zeroed in on where the intruders stood.

Dan and Tom fled back through the tunnel – their mission accomplished. Several scouts now clattered over the boulders in pursuit, and roaring up behind them was the enraged Bull.

Retreating the way they came, Dan and Tom dropped more fume-bombs – clouding the beasts' vision. They entered the feeding den and paused to scatter the last of their bombs.

Back near the large boulders, the propane tank in Tom's pyre was glowing red. In the next instant, it *exploded!* The smoke billowed up to the cavern roof, expanded, and then fell.

The heavy fumes from the flaming insecticide-soaked rubber swiftly fouled the air. Now, all of the scorpions in the nest – large and small – dashed about, suffocating.

Hearing the pursuing scorpions closing in, Dan and Tom dashed into the front tunnel.

The fumes continued to spread throughout the caverns and deep into the nest. One scorpion tried backing into the cave's recesses but simply could not escape the fumes. Another beast jumped out from a narrow crevice – its body quaking, in desperate need of fresh air. The monsters had no choice but to flee the caverns and head towards the fissure opening.

Dan and Tom flew through the front tunnel, past their now-dying road flares. As the scorpions behind them dashed out of the feeding den, the Bull furiously pushed his way to the lead – bolting through the front tunnel with Dan and Tom in his sights.

Nearing the fissure opening, the two men tore off their respirators.

Dan lifted his flare gun and shouted, "We're headed out!"

Chapter 25

▶ Dan and Tom dashed from the fissure into the moonlight. As they ran up the slope of the pit, Dan shot a flare straight upward.

"They're right behind us!" cried Tom.

Dan yelled, "Linda, wait for my signal!"

On top of the tower, under the fading glow of the flare, Linda moved closer to the knife switch. She placed her hand on the lever and looked down.

Tom joined Anne at the hilltop, near the second electrode. But Dan ran straight up the center of the hill, past the electrodes. He paused at the front edge of the firetrap area and turned to face the fissure.

The droning grew louder and Dan raised his arms. "Get ready!"

With a deafening hiss, the Bull Scorpion tore through the opening. Dan waved his arms and yelled taunts from the front edge of the firetrap.

And, as the Bull rushed straight up the center of the pit, Dan dropped his hands. "NOW!"

Linda threw the switch, and the timing couldn't have been better.

As the Bull set foot between the conductors, a bright blue electric arc crackled to life – catching the beast dead-on, stopping him in his tracks. He arched back, shrieking, and shook violently.

Dan backed up and climbed behind the first electrode to join Yoli.

The Bull Scorpion's shell cracked and shriveled. Ooze burst from his joints, and his eyes exploded! In an instant, the monster curled up into a still, charred mess.

Two more scouts dashed out of the fissure. While the first scout – like the Bull – was caught in the arc, the second scorpion sensed the danger and tried to turn around.

With Billy reloading for them, Patrick and Jennie fired their flare guns. The scorpion stepped backwards, barely dodging the

134

flares. And as Dan and Tom added their rifle fire from both sides of the hilltop, the beast was forced backwards, into the arc.

Two more scorpions scurried from the fissure.

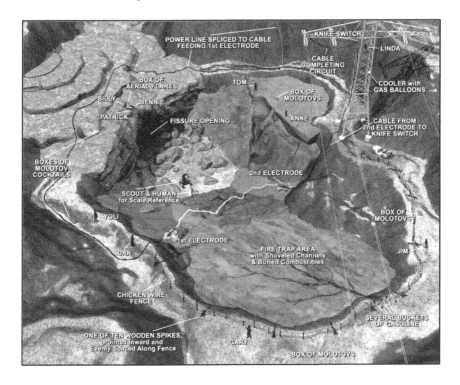

One beast turned and began climbing the rocks just above the opening – inadvertently heading for Patrick, Jennie, and Billy. Dan and Tom opened fire with their rifles, but to no avail. While running to their children's aid, the men didn't notice the second scorpion heading straight up the hill at Yoli.

Yoli aimed her rifle and fired at the monster, but the beast closed in.

Dropping the Marlin, Yoli raised her shotgun. "Alright, you fucker, eat *this!*" She fired.

The slug splattered the creature's head, causing it to topple backwards towards the fissure. It landed, writhing, on its back.

Dan and Tom joined the kids in firing at the climbing scorpion. The beast lost its footing and fell onto its writhing brother.

▶ Inside the caverns, Dan's time-delay fuse had burned its way to his pyre. The pile burst into flames, spewing up more toxic smoke.

▶ As the scorpion that Yoli shot died in the pit, the other scout remained on its back, too – thrashing. Pushing with its tail, the beast tried to upright itself. But Dan and Tom blasted it with their rifles, pulverizing its underside.

Patrick pointed. "Their shell's softer underneath!"

"Indeed, it *is!*" agreed Dan.

Another two scorpions nimbly scurried out of the opening. The first beast paused just in front of the arc, but the second one bumped him into it. As the first beast fried, the second managed to step over him – just missing being zapped. He entered the firetrap area.

From the rear center of the fence, Gary and Jim saw the beast evade the arc. So they poured two buckets of gasoline into the canal they'd dug earlier. The fuel flowed down towards the advancing monster and also into the side channels. Though the beast tried to take in fresh air, the fumes from the gasoline filled its book-lungs.

From her position on the tower, Linda focused on that scorpion and moved down to the cooler. She raised the lid, grabbed a gas balloon, and tossed it downward. The balloon burst directly on the scorpion's head, in back of its eyes.

Three more scorpions exited the fissure. With flare-fire forcing him up the hill, the first beast was zapped in the arc. The second one turned around to see what was attacking them and was met head-on with rifle fire. The third monster stumbled over the frying first beast to join the other scorpion in the firetrap area.

Linda tossed a gas-balloon at *this* scorpion, as well. It missed and splashed onto the ground. She tossed another, striking the back of its tail.

Now, the two scorpions inside the firetrap area began to slowly crawl towards its center.

"Hawh! Hawh!" Gary waved his arms and shouted taunts at the first one.

The beast turned to face him then took a step forward.

"HAWH!" Gary positioned himself immediately behind one of the long spikes, and the scorpion charged.

136

"Yeah, come 'n get me!" Gary raised his flare gun.

Rushing forward, the beast impaled itself on the spike. Gary fired a flare, igniting the fuel on its head. Berserk, the monster stumbled back.

In the pit between the fissure and the arc, the combined rifle fire of Dan, Tom, Yoli, and Anne finished off the two remaining scorpions. There was a momentary pause. Three more beasts were hesitating, just inside the fissure opening.

▶ Deep in the tunnel, the red-hot tank in Dan's pyre exploded! As the blast echoed, a shockwave of fumes punched through the caverns in every direction.

▶ A gust of smoke surged from the fissure. To avoid the fumes, the three scorpions now dashed out into the pit. Patrick and Jennie blasted them with flares.

The first beast turned, dodged two flares, and backed into the crackling arc. The other two scorpions turned and scrambled. But they, too, were forced upwards by the flare and rifle fire.

As the current shot through the first scorpion, the third beast backed across his brother's frying carcass and entered the firetrap area. The second monster crossed to the side of the pit, trying to avoid the gunfire.

Linda tossed two more gas balloons.

While the third monster careened towards the others in the firetrap area, the balloons hit the ground near them.

Several yards away, the flames on the carapace of the burning scorpion were nearly out – yet the beast still lived!

Seeing Gary and Jim, one of the scorpions charged towards the fence and was stabbed by a spike. Wounded, it backed away.

The third scorpion paused, carefully eyeing the situation.

▶ Back in the caverns, the monsters that remained in the nest were in a total panic. The toxic smoke had flowed into the deepest crannies and rebounded off the walls. Now rising, the swirling fumes forced the last holdouts upward – including one final horror from the deepest recess.

▶ As smoke continued to billow from the fissure, two more scorpions dashed into the pit. Moving up the hill at full tilt, the first one was caught directly in the arc. The second beast panicked and turned. But a flare-blast startled the monster backwards – past the current.

Linda tossed another balloon, and it splashed onto the second scorpion's head. The beast whipped around, enraged – trying to see what had hit him.

Now, the four scorpions creeping about the firetrap area were quaking – gasping for air.

Gary met Jim at the back of the fence. "Think we have enough?"

"Yep," replied Jim, with a glint in his eye. "Let's *broil* 'em!"

They tipped more of the gasoline buckets, and the fuel rushed down through the shoveled channels.

Jim handed Gary a Molotov cocktail and lit the end. Gary flung the flaming jar into the center of the firetrap, where it burst and ignited the fuel.

The flames swiftly spread through the canals. And, as the heat seared their outer shells, the four scorpions flew into a frenzy.

The planted combustibles caught fire, and the flames grew higher. Jim and Gary moved down opposite sides of the fence – flare guns raised and ready.

Trying to escape the flames, one scorpion made a dash towards the fence. Jim fired a flare – just grazing its carapace – and the beast halted. On the other side of the trap, another monster charged at Gary, but a flare bursting on its head sent it backwards.

One by one, the buried gasbags began to explode. Large flames soared upward, and the four scorpions were engulfed in a firestorm.

▶ Meanwhile, the only beast alive in the front pit had moved near the fissure opening. Everyone saw that one of its pinchers had been sliced into two pieces.

"That's Al's work," shouted Dan, as he racked his shotgun and took aim. "And this one's for *him!*"

As Dan's slug blew off one of its legs, the beast was caught in Tom, Yoli, and Anne's rifle fire. Growing weak, the monster stumbled backwards. And Patrick and Jennie fired their flares – forcing it uphill into the current.

Now, the space between the fissure and the arc was littered with the bodies of twelve dead scorpions.

For a moment, nothing came from the opening. Then, more smoke bellowed outward – followed by two more scorpions.

Again, Patrick and Jennie blasted them with flares.

While the first scorpion was caught in the arc, the second beast stepped past the current. But as he set foot in the firetrap, the flames flared up before him. To avoid the heat, the monster backed up – right into the arc – and fried.

▶ Fervidly, Gary lit another Molotov and moved close to the fence. He flung the jar. But his movement caught the eye of a scorpion hovering behind nearby flames. Enraged, the monster charged – stretching its legs to gain height.

Gary raised his flare gun but, before he could fire, the beast reached over the fence and seized him. As the pincher crushed his ribs, Gary writhed – dropping his weapons.

The beast pulled Gary into the firetrap and, in a fury, stung him repeatedly. With each whip of its tail, the scorpion's venom shot into the air and sizzled in the flames. Gary's screams died away. His clothing began to burn.

Dan and Jim ran up to the fence – Jim with his rifle, Dan with his shotgun. But it was too late. Gary twitched one last time and went limp.

The beast saw the two men. It lifted Gary, taunting them, then charged.

Firing their guns, Jim shot out the beast's eyes while Dan's slug took off its head. The monster recoiled and crumbled to the ground, dropping Gary. The boy's burning body rolled to a halt, and one of his own gas bags – buried just below – exploded!

Dan impulsively started forward, but Jim grabbed his shoulder – shaking his head. As the two men backed away, the flames in the firetrap peaked. Every being within was reduced to ash.

Dan and Jim grabbed the remaining gas buckets and Molotovs and headed towards the front pit.

▶ While a solitary scorpion was being forced back into the arc, Jim and Dan brought the buckets around the edge of the pit to join Anne.

At that point, another wave of smoke surged from the fissure, and seven infant scorpions scurried out from the opening.

"What the–?!" exclaimed Anne.

Dan acknowledged, "It's their young!"

Two of the confused infants ran into the arc and were broiled.

The others desperately sought a cleft to hide under. Two tried to dash back into the fissure but were stopped by Patrick and Jennie's flares.

Tom joined Dan and Jim, and they tossed the three buckets into the pit – splashing gasoline all over the young beasts. Patrick and Jennie fired two more flares, igniting the fuel. For good measure, the men tossed in several Molotovs. And the young scorpions were trapped in a small inferno.

As the flames in the firetrap area died down, the flames in the pit hit their peak.

One of the young scorpions backed away from the flames and into the arc.

Two of the young monsters tried climbing the walls. Jennie and Patrick shot flares at them, and one fell back into the pit. Once on its back, the young scorpion's underside was blasted to pulp by rifle fire.

Another infant tried scaling the wall.

Dan and Tom fired their flare guns, and the two climbers were knocked down.

Then, Dan emptied his rifle into the remaining young – as did Tom, Yoli, Anne, and Jim. And the young scorpions succumbed to the gunfire and flames.

Without buried kindling, the pit fire – fueled only by the gasoline – was already burning out.

Everyone lowered their weapons. Patrick, Jennie, and Billy cringed as the flames died, revealing a vista of charred, dead scorpions.

Now, the only sound was that of the electric arc.

Looking down from the tower, Linda shouted, "Dan?!"

Dan stared for a few moments at the fissure then looked-up and waved at Linda. "Okay, cut it!"

She threw the switch, and the arc shut off.

Those on the ground stepped forward – their eyes riveted on the opening. Up on the tower, Linda climbed down a few rungs for a better view.

Dan, Tom, Yoli, Jim, Anne, Patrick, Jennie, and Billy began to relax.

"I hope that's it," said Jennie, turning to Patrick.

"It better be. Our ammo's nearly gone."

Dan and Tom cautiously stepped down into the pit. Part way, they paused – peering deep into the blackness of the opening.

Nothing.

Chapter 26

▶ Tom smiled and faced Dan.

But Dan was still on guard – his eyes fixed on the fissure. "There's something–"

With a thunderous hiss, the mother of all scorpions – a 25-foot Queen – slowly stepped out of the opening and paused. Terrified, everyone backed away. Tom discharged his rifle, but it was like firing a pea shooter at a bus.

"Linda, hit the switch!" yelled Dan as he and Tom ran up the hill. "Turn it back on!"

Linda clambered up to the lever.

The Queen saw Dan fleeing and started towards him. Crawling up out of the pit, her right foreleg came down on the first electrode just as Linda pulled the switch.

The beast's foot smacked the conductor from the rocks. The current zapped into the ground. And a bolt of plasma shot up the cable to the tower – fraying the insulation.

As Linda pulled her hand away, the switch blew apart in a shower of sparks. The power cable dropped to the ground. Linda lost her footing and fell, but her safety harness snapped taught.

This caught the Queen's attention, and she halted. The image of Linda swinging, unconscious, at the end of her safety line reflected off her bulbous eyes.

As the Queen headed towards Linda, Dan and Tom ran forward – shotguns blasting! The monster reached the tower and began scaling it.

Seeing this, Jennie dashed to the box of Molotovs and grabbed the last one.

With the slugs proving useless, Dan lowered his shotgun to see the Queen closing in on Linda. "*No!*" Desperate, Dan dashed back to grab the first electrode and bolted forward – swinging the cable above his head like a lasso and hurling it.

The electrode hit the top of the Queen's tail and the cable wrapped around it, just below her stinger. As Dan yanked, Tom

142

and Jim grabbed the cable behind him to help. The tugging enraged the Queen, and she stopped.

The three men pulled even harder.

"Come on, you bitch!" screamed Dan. "Come on down and pick on me!"

The Queen turned and lunged downward.

As the others scattered, Dan stood his ground. He raised his shotgun and fired, but the beast wasn't fazed. Dan backed up – the Queen darting straight for him.

Jennie handed the last Molotov to Tom. "Your arm's stronger than mine!"

As Tom reached for his lighter, Jim fired his flare gun at the Queen.

The flare only grazed the beast's carapace, but it slowed her enough to buy Dan a few seconds more.

Tom lit the Molotov and flung it.

The Queen dodged the firebomb, and it burst onto the sand.

With the monster closing in, Dan got off two more slugs before his ammo was spent. The beast flinched when hit, but she didn't stop. Dan then flung his empty shotgun at her eyes and drew Al's sword from his belt.

Rushing forward, the Queen shot out her left pincher. Dan hacked into it with the sword. As he stabbed it again, the beast swung around her right pincher and seized him.

Then, she launched her tail forward – her stinger shooting for Dan's chest.

Dan cocked Al's sword and swung. He severed the stinger from the tail and sent it flying into the pit.

Furious, the monster raised Dan towards her jaws. But Dan lifted his flare gun and fired straight into her mouth. The rocket exploded, and the Queen lurched backwards – pulling Dan away from her face.

Seizing the moment, Dan hacked at the pincher with Al's sword. The beast dropped him, and he dashed beneath her.

In a fury, Dan thrust the sword straight up into the Queen's belly!

She shrieked out an ear-splitting hiss and tried to back away.

Dan ripped the sword out then rammed it up again – deeper!

The Queen went berserk.

Fighting against her lurches and coarse shell, Dan forced Al's sword down the length of the beast's underbelly – slicing her open and spilling her guts!

The Queen curled in agony then lost her footing. As she collapsed into a twitching dying mess, Dan stepped out from underneath. He staggered forward, covered in goo.

Patrick, Jennie, Billy, Jim, and Anne gathered around – gazing in awe at Dan and the vanquished giant. At the tower, Tom and Yoli were retrieving Linda.

"Dad!" Jennie ran to Dan and hugged him – goo and all – then yanked off her sweater to wipe him down.

Tom and Yoli approached, supporting Linda, who was weak but okay. Linda looked up at her husband, smiled, then collapsed in his arms.

For the first time in two days, everyone could breathe easily. Weary, they stumbled towards their vehicles – leaving the devastation in the battleground behind them.

Epilogue

▶ The Montgomerys, Hernandezes, and Johnsons remained at the campgrounds for one more day – exhausting the last of their supplies.

That morning, Dan and Tom drove Al's Land-Ranger up and down Highway 18. The Sand Canyon Bridge remained down, with nothing – save for the flashing barricade – visible beyond it. No patrol cars or officers had arrived. And, at Dead Man's Pass, the rockslide had yet to be cleared.

In the afternoon, donning gloves and respirators, Dan, Tom, and Linda tackled the grim task of bagging any remains they could find and placing them in the shed. Not everyone who'd fallen victim to the scorpions could be accounted for – but the survivors did their best to identify whomever they could.

Late that afternoon, with mobile phone service still down, Jennie fished Michael's boom box from the Reyes' trailer and tuned into Buddy Maxwell's newscasts.

On hearing the reports, Dan surmised that they'd soon be rescued.

▶ The next morning, Linda rose early and began sweeping the Winnebago in the hope of soon leaving. Bumping over one of Dan's boots, she was startled to see a small yellow desert scorpion crawl out of it.

"Well, hi there, little Vaejovis Spinogerus. Don't know how you got in here, but you'd better not let my hubby find you."

Dan groggily turned over in his sleep. "Huh, whaaa?!"

"Nothing, dear," chuckled Linda. "Go back to sleep."

She gently brushed the tiny critter onto her road map, took it outside, and set it on the ground by some boulders. "There. Head on home, now."

At that moment, as the little scorpion scuttled under the rocks, a search helicopter came buzzing overhead from the East. The noise awakened everyone else, and they rushed out to wave as it circled above and then flew back the way it came.

145

▶ Two hours later, a set of bulldozers had cleared the rockslide on 18, and a State Police car cruised into the park. As Dan and Linda greeted them, the officers saw the overturned super coach, the damaged Reyes trailer, and Al's demolished kitchen window. Being shirtless, Dan sported the bruises he'd garnered from the Queen's grip.

"You look beat!" observed the First Trooper.

"And *you're* a sight for sore eyes," replied Dan.

The Second Trooper asked, "What the devil happened here?!"

"As they say, *it's a long story*. But first, would you please call out the nearest coroner?"

"And uh, a zoology team from the nearest college would be a big help too!" added Linda.

"Say what?!" The Second Trooper gazed at her, baffled.

▶ After a few more hours, Tom was assisting the three-man team from the coroner's office. Just outside of Al's shed, they placed bag after bag on the ground in front of their van.

"Holy mother!" cried the Chief Coroner – his professional demeanor cracking for the first time in his career. "I've seen a lot, but nothing *ever* like this!"

"*And*," Tom raised his palm then pointed at the trailheads, "there's likely more remains out *there* that we haven't come across!"

The coroner looked Tom in the eye. "Wha'd you say did this?"

Tom shook his head. "We *didn't* say. But you'll see soon enough ... and you'll wish you hadn't."

▶ At the fissure site, Linda was aiding a zoology team from U.C.-Riverside.

And Dan had just finished telling the whole story to the Troopers. "So now you see why we wouldn't say *exactly* what had attacked us – not until you'd seen all this."

"Well, if you think that we'd 've considered you ripe for the loony bin," the First Trooper sighed, "you're probably right."

"But let's face it," the Second Trooper added while crossing to the gutted carcass of the Queen Scorpion. "Ya can't argue with *this!*"

"You certainly can't, m'boy," said elderly, erudite Professor Harold Medford II, while crouched on the ground examining the carcass. He stood and faced the Troopers. "No hoax here, officers. It's a genuine *Thunder Scorpion* – the *Brontoscorpio* of the Paleozoic – alive today. Amazing! ... Much *larger* than believed, too!" Medford shook his head then turned to Dan. "What you had to do was regrettable, but I understand. It's ... it's just ... that ... having a *live* one would have been so wonderful."

"Wonderful?!" exclaimed Dan.

"I assure you, Dr. Medford," retorted Linda as she joined the men, "after what we've seen, you wouldn't *dare* try to wrangle a live one!"

"No, my dear. You're quite right," Medford agreed – visions of academic sugarplums fading from his eyes.

▶ Later, back at the campgrounds, the Troopers had gathered everyone's statement and contact info.

"Look, after all you've been through, we won't detain you any longer," the First Trooper said to Dan, Tom, and Jim. "You've ID'd the victims. And Cal-Ed's on its way to restore the grid."

"Medford's team 'll likely determine how these creatures survived all this time," advised the Second Trooper, "and there's really nothing more you can add."

The First Trooper nodded. "We'll phone if we need to ask anything else."

"Well, thank you," said a relieved Tom – Dan and Jim agreeing.

"Look, before heading back east, we're all checking into Serrano for a day or two," volunteered Dan, "so we'll be *there* if you need us. Just ... keep our names out of the news, okay?"

"Oh yeah," the Troopers nodded, "no problem!"

At one of the nearby picnic tables, Patrick was reviewing his printouts with Dr. Medford – excitedly waving his arms as he told him what they'd been able to determine.

And Medford listened intently – smiling and nodding – knowing that the boy had called it correctly. "I think maybe a previously undiscovered genus, Patrick – one *descending* from Brontoscorpio but growing larger in the oxygen-rich air of the Carboniferous. Like their smaller cousins, *Pulmonoscorpius*, your

scorpions also had larger eyes – ideal for aggressive, visually-
oriented hunting."

▶ In a few moments, the Montgomerys, Hernandezes, and
Johnsons pulled their vehicles up to the park's main gate.

"So head south to 10," Tom shouted to Dan and Jim, "then go
west about 25 miles, and the resort 'll be on your right."

"Sounds heavenly," said Linda.

"Our card balance be damned," proclaimed Dan, "we've all
earned a good night's sleep in a decent hotel!"

"Here-here!" agreed Jim.

As everyone cheered, they drove down the gravel road to 18,
hung a right, and bade their final farewells to Desert Rocks.

▶ A hot shower and change of clothes later, the nine of them sat
around a large circular table in the central restaurant of the Serrano
Casino Resort.

Dan was planted between Linda and Jennie – an arm around
each. Patrick – his arm also around Jennie – smiled proudly. With
the tension gone, they were now just one exhausted family that was
happy to be alive.

Billy quietly sat next to Patrick – Tom and Yoli beside him.

And Jim and Anne were cuddled together – smooching as
giddily as two high-school sweethearts.

As a young, grinning waitress arrived with stiff drinks for the
adults and sodas for the kids, a busboy doled out the menus.

"Give us a while to peruse these, okay?" requested Dan. "Gotta
chill a bit, first."

"I understand," the unflappably cheerful waitress retorted
before disappearing.

"If only she *really* knew," offered Anne. She turned to Jim and
took his hand. "I'm so thankful we got through it."

"As Jennie would likely say," chimed Jim while lifting his
drink, "*it's been real!*"

"Yeah," Jennie nervously laughed, "a real *nightmare!*"

"But that's just it," Tom added. "I mean ... sitting here, right
now ... it all seems like a bad dream."

Dan nodded. "Well, I have to admit that the extent of what's
happened is really just *now* hitting me."

"PTSD for all of us," said Yoli.

"No kidding, Mom!" Billy finally opened up, "I'm not sure I'll ever sleep again."

"Me neither," added Jennie.

"That'll pass in time," assured Dan. "But, for a while, we'll *all* be jumpin' at any bump in the night!"

After a sober moment of silence, Tom raised his glass. "To our friends who didn't make it!"

"Yes," agreed Dan, "to the heroes that didn't survive."

As everyone joined in the toast, the waitress returned, check-pad in hand, "Okay, folks, you ready?"

"Ah, sorry," said Dan, "we've just been sittin' here jawin'."

Linda smiled. "Have ya anything on special?"

"Sure do! How do barbeque ribs sound?"

Everyone's face fell.

"Girl," retorted Anne, "we've seen enough *ribs* to last us a lifetime. What else you got?"

Unflinchingly, the waitress suggested, "Well, we have some seafood specials?"

Linda perked up. "Oh, I would kill for some good salmon!"

"Well, sorry. We're fresh outta fish," the waitress admitted. But with incorrigible enthusiasm, she beamed a huge smile and cheerfully asked, "But whaddaya say to *steamed lobster* or *king crab legs*?!"

APPENDIX – CAST GALLERY

FULL-LENGTH PORTRAITS OF
THE PRINCIPAL CHARACTERS

As Dressed for Robert and Lauri's Engagement Party

DAN MONTGOMERY

LINDA MONTGOMERY

PATRICK MONTGOMERY

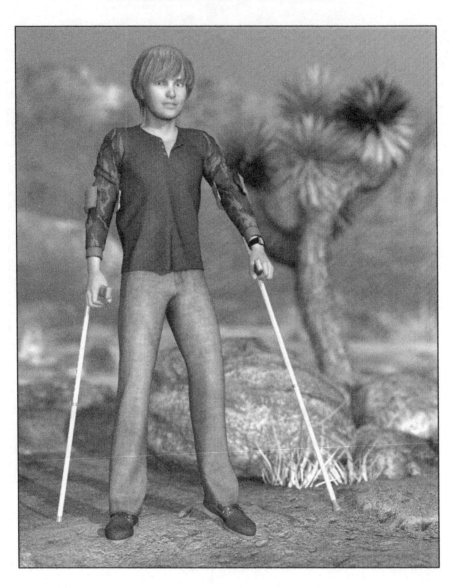

JENNIE MONTGOMERY

TOM HERNANDEZ

YOLI HERNANDEZ

BILLY HERNANDEZ

AL NISHIDA

ROBERT NISHIDA

LAURI YOUNG

KEN YOUNG

JOYCE YOUNG

MICHAEL REYES

ELAINE REYES

FRANK STEWART

MARGARET STEWART

JIM JOHNSON

ANNE JOHNSON

STEVE LACY

MITCH DAVIS

KATHY SMITH

DAVID GROGAN

GARY ARCHER

About the author

DAVID V. GREGORY's earliest childhood memory is of being planted in front of an old Philco TV and delighting over the first Black & White Looney Tunes ever syndicated to local stations. Not only did those vintage Porky and Daffy shorts nurture his sense of humor, but that exposure to the work of Tex Avery, Bob Clampett, and Frank Tashlin began wiring Dave's young brain in the techniques of visual storytelling. In grade school, Dave found himself making 8mm animated cartoons. And while in high school – inspired by the films of Don Chaffey, Ray Harryhausen, and others – Dave created 20-minute 16mm sci-fi epics with self-executed visual effects.

After receiving his Bachelor's Degree in Motion Picture Production from Southern Illinois University, Dave began his Hollywood career as an Optical Special-Effects Cameraman at Ray Mercer & Company. In those pre-digital days, while employed with Mercer's, Pacific Title, and other studios, Dave contributed optical special effects for numerous features, television programs, and commercials – including the original STAR WARS, STAR TREK THE MOTION PICTURE, HANGAR 18, LEAPIN' LEPRECHAUNS, THE ARRIVAL, and QUEST OF THE DELTA KNIGHTS (yes, those plasma comets that blew-up David Warner at the end were actually Dave's own hand-drawn animation). A few years later, Dave transitioned into the digital realm as the Supervising Colorist for Warner Digital Studio's flying saucer and global destruction effects on MARS ATTACKS.

Throughout his visual effects career, Dave never stopped writing, making short films, and creating traditional & CG art – all under the auspices of his d/b/a, Galaxie Entertainment Company. Since 2003, Dave concentrated his efforts solely on his own ventures, while retaining the artistic sensibilities he developed in the hands-on analog days.

For the Fall/Winter 2007 issue of CAMERA OPERATOR Magazine, he wrote and illustrated the popular and controversial article, "Stereoscopic 3-D Cinema – Another Cycle or Here to Stay?"

Recently, Dave adapted ATTACK OF THE BLACK SCORPIONS from his original screenplay, "SCORPIONS!" And now, with the pandemic finally winding down, Dave is focused on making the feature film version of this story. He can be reached by email at *galaxiefilm@post.com* .

Acknowledgements

Eternal gratitude for the guidance and support of my three editors –
Gary W. Adkins, Imogen Grace Evans, and Peter Tulipan. Peter
and Gary helped steer me, chapter by chapter, through the
novelization's first and subsequent drafts. And Imogen tackled the
final pre-press edit with amazing speed and accuracy. The old
saying, "couldn't have done it without you," couldn't be more
applicable than here.

Regarding the Illustrations

The front & back covers, character portraits, and other illustrations
for this novel were executed by the author using POSER PRO and
GIMP software – with CG models and photographic assets under
standard and extended commercial licenses from Renderosity,
RuntimeDNA, HiveWire3D, TurboSquid, CG Bytes, ShareCG,
PoserWorld, CGtrader, 3Dexport, Most Digital Creations,
Shutterstock, Content Paradise, Daz-3D, and Adobe Stock.
Sincere thanks to all of the individual vendors, and a very special
thank you to Bondware for rescuing one of the finest CG programs
ever created.

Get your *Free*
ATTACK OF THE BLACK SCORPIONS
"Prelude" Teaser Comix

Good-day, folks! Dave Gregory, here.

Not long ago, I created a short Teaser Comic-Book of my novel's opening "Prelude" sequence. And I would love to send it to you as a free PDF copy.

To receive your Teaser-Comix, please place your full name and email address in the body of a message and send it by email to...
galaxiefilm@post.com . *

Oh, and please, type *"Requesting Teaser Comix"* into the subject line.

Also, if you have a moment to add a quick note, it would help me to know the format you read my book in – whether it be Paperback, Hardback, ePub, on a Kindle device, or in Kindle format on a Tablet or Phone.

Thank you very much, and I look forward to hearing from you!

Dave

179

Made in the USA
Monee, IL
09 January 2025

76471313R00111